In Her words

T.J. THOMPSON

ISBN: 978-0-646-97722-5

In Her Words

T.J. THOMPSON

To my family,

I love you.

To those who encouraged me to
do what makes my heart sing,
I thank you.

CHAPTER ONE

Butterflies dancing in her Belly

I adored you ever since the first moment I first saw you. Your gleaming eyes and gorgeous smile. Your lips so smooth, I could not bear to look away. You made my heart glimmer and with every breath I took you catapulted me to another realm, just with the power of your smile. You tore the covers away from my soul and from there you began to mess with my head. You unbuttoned my blouse to expose my heart. Sadly, you took it out and forgot to return it when you left.

You bastard.

Look at what you've done to me.

Forever never yours,

Rose

With anguish, Sasha thrashed at her manuscript. Her mind firmly on the suffocating blanket of deep hurt that had encouraged her raw, yet powerful prologue. Sasha's main character, 'Rose' gave her a voice unlike her own; a sense of expression she could only ever entertain via this literary form. Perhaps a confessional of sorts, Sasha's book of journals had always delivered a gift; the ability to express freely, without the worry of judgement. Of course, this excluded the judgement she would continually place on herself. It was only ever meant for her eyes until a fire in her belly erupted; the kind of fire one only feels when they've been through hell.

Was it all true?

When he tore her heart out?

When he ripped it to shreds?

There was nothing cut and dry about the story she would go on to share. It was long, complex and brutally honest. Time had passed yet still, these memories caused shivers to tingle down Sasha's weathered spine. This woman, who over time had gathered the strength of a thousand men, would have never been able to get through all this unscathed; undamaged by the twists and turns of a troublesome life. Peering through a looking glass at what was to come, well that could not be possible. Sasha had to walk through it all and often she'd fall, get up and dust herself off; all with the hope that someday she may soar. Within this woman lay a deep amalgamation of emotions; windswept happiness, gut-wrenching hurt and bottomless shame. For her life had been far from simple.

Did the 'he' in her story cause all of this?

Or was Sasha the captain of her own fate?

It would take her almost an entire lifetime to figure that out.

'Rose', her fictional muse quickly became the messenger of all things true that lay buried beneath the surface. Her words, perhaps sometimes quite punishing, steered Sasha through some of the toughest terrain she would ever conquer. This was all about Sasha; her words, her life. Her journey.

'Take me forth, into a world of the

unknown and shadow me with your wisdom. Listen, I will. Yet only from time to time. For this is my road to roam; it is my life to build. It's my life to fuck up, and if I do, I won't let it get me down. None of us will get through this life without making a mess sometimes.'

Sasha told herself that it wasn't at all necessary to add this small yet slightly mature excerpt; words she recorded before leaving home during her late teens. Yet she added them in anyway, as a little reminder of how her thoughts would have evolved over the years. She'd kept this journal, in her early, headstrong, yet careless 'flitter my life away' days. It was handwritten, which was unusual given that computers, smartphones and all that jazz kept most others in this generation from picking up a pencil. Sasha's attitude back then would provide her full access to do whatever she wanted; when she wanted. And just like this paragraph suggested, she understood consequence as a 'thing' from quite a young age. However, knowing and actually facing consequence didn't always go hand in hand. Sasha seemed untouchable, and so from the day she left her childhood home, and as life kept throwing her jewel after jewel, she bathed in all the riches that would fall seamlessly at her feet. Here was a young woman who had it all together. The beginnings of a promising career, the confidence, the looks, and the man; that man who would go on to tear her heart out. A slightly flawed, yet fairly close to perfect life. Or so it seemed.

Her naivety would go on to be poked and prodded, until that very naivety that got her this far, would transform into pure strength. Because it had to. As Sasha had predicted, she would go onto slip up. No *one* person could ever live this kind of charmed existence forever.

So, life away from home began just as rosy as one could imagine.

Sasha arrived as a simple, down to earth young woman from the country, cementing herself slap bang in the chaos of a bustling metropolis; a total contrast to her humble beginnings. She transformed herself into somewhat of an urbanite, wearing up to date fashions, relishing in every chance to schmooze in the city's exclusive social scene. Having all the right contacts had suddenly become a priority to this country girl, and by using those associations, this vivacious young woman was destined to climb her custom-made career ladder in record time. You see, Sasha's small-town charm ensured she would always keep her manners – *most of the time*. She would never step on anybody else's tail – unless she had to, and most prevalent of all, Sasha would always strive to make her own way. There were to be no shortcuts for this country gal. Those who knew Sasha before her re-birth into a hip city chick would remember her as the tousled haired blonde beauty, wearing the dirty jeans and dusty boots who was, like most women on the land, raised as tough as nails (and not to mention every cowboys dream.)

She was the daughter of third-generation wheat farmers who lived and worked the land in country New South Wales. So, in essence, Sasha had traded out her roots for city lights, changing everything about herself with exception to her well-bred nature and witty personality.

These days, her wardrobe consisted of everything but those dirty jeans. Her hair had changed, to a sharp, straight cut, she'd never leave her apartment without her 'face' on and Sasha maintained the biggest shoe collection that one could squeeze into her median-sized studio apartment closet.

Her appearance may have seen quite a transformation though Sasha remained a beautiful, carefree soul on the inside. That attribute was what made her stand apart from the rest. Sasha was just a free spirit who had worked hard to open her own doors, and the city was where she needed to be to see her dreams come true. Exactly what defined those dreams was beginning to become vague to Sasha. She had the blossoming career, the boyfriend and the friends. Was she fulfilled in every way? Well that's a story for another day.

Her journal quickly became her therapy, a way of unloading and unpacking her feelings so that they would no longer weigh her down. A man with whom she imagined a lifetime with, all before he suddenly left, featured heavily and deservedly so.

Dr. Keir Sterling, was his name. A seemingly rich and

successful almost middle-aged man with the confidence to match. Sasha liked that Keir was the kind of guy who would sweep her off her feet in a flashy kind of way, unlike anyone else before him. She was relatively inexperienced (and as previously mentioned, a touch naïve) with only a high school romance prior. Yet Keir provoked a naturally tranquil weakness in her. To Sasha, that weakness felt like love.

They met on a balmy evening at an inner-city and ultra-trendy garden market. You know, the kinds where every second stall reads 'organic' and where a multitude of equally cool people lay scattered on open lawn; drinking cool cider whilst listening to an equally fashionable band.

There he was. Standing by the pop up bar to the side of the stage. The music was loud yet not too deafening that one couldn't hold a conversation. Sasha stood there sipping her iced tea from a straw. She kept glancing over, keeping a casual eye on the well-dressed man as he went from standing tall to scuttling to find whatever it was that he'd just dropped into the grass below. He looked as though he had arrived straight from the office, still in his day suit. But it was a Sunday. Sasha's eyes drew toward him like a magnet; there were no other people like him at this market. Everybody was just so casual, relaxed and basking in the warm afternoon sunlight. Yet here was this guy, buying one of those trendy ciders that seemed to be all the rage. Sasha kept looking over at the man, as she browsed a nearby stall. By this time, there he was, on all fours, frantically searching through what seemed like every blade of grass. So frantic, that he'd urged people to move away so he could capture a clearer view. A moment passed and as Sasha peered back over toward the man, a square of paper blew aimlessly in her direction. She lent down to pick it up and noticed it was a photo of a woman printed on office paper, yet before she could look too closely at the image, the man quickly approached and snatched it from her grasp.

"Thank you" he said softly. "That belongs to me."

Their eyes locked.

As instant as a click of the fingers, Sasha felt something. Butterflies, nerves, the pound of her heart – or all three. His piercing blue eyes and charming face lured Sasha in. He truly wasn't her type, yet still she felt an attraction.

'What about the photo? He's probably with someone!' said the hysterical over-thinking voice inside Sasha's head.

'But he is so handsome – what if he's not?' she thought, succumbing to her innate urge to not turn and walk away.

"Anyway, thanks for picking it up" said the tall stranger, as he oddly bounced his eyes between Sasha and the mystery picture.

It was at this point that Sasha noticed his enticing English accent. And if that wasn't enough, those striking blue eyes were still staring right at her in such a mesmerizing way, that Sasha found herself deeply intrigued by the fine-looking stranger. It was almost as though they knew each other from somewhere.

With butterflies dancing in her belly, Sasha felt that that there was no walking away from this. And these thoughts and emotions catapulted Sasha's mind like a tsunami; in time that felt like a cliché, paused blissfully still.

Searching for a reason to speak, Sasha spotted in the distance that the man had forgotten something.

"You forgot your drink" she kindly mentioned, pointing and guiding his eye to his cider, still sitting alone on the bar.

"Oh yes. I must confess that this isn't my usual scene. I just stopped here on the way home" explained the man, almost tripping over his words.

"I'm sorry, this is so rude of me. My name is Keir. Keir Sterling. I'm the weird and rightfully awkward guy who just snatched something from you without explaining. I do apologise. It's truly nice to meet you."

Sasha smiled, totally falling for his quirky effort at humour and that accent; that incredibly alluring accent.

"It's fine. I'm Sasha by the way, and I'm clearly underdressed" she replied with a smile, looking Keir up and down.

He chuckled, clearly getting her joke. Here was Keir, wearing a designer-grade suit and tie, and there was Sasha, wearing her casual best, shorts and a crochet top. Sasha's transition from city to country hadn't completely filtered through to the weekends just yet, though at least she had done away with those dirty jeans.

Like a classic gentleman, Keir reached out his right hand. His touch seemed to momentarily wake those nervous flutters that kept bouncing around in the pit of her stomach. They were strong, and so was his grasp, yet in a comforting kind of way. Sasha instantly knew that this wasn't a normal 'how do you do' kind of meeting. There was something that intrigued her about this man as she looked up at his face and all she wanted to do at that very moment was to know more, see more; feel more. Sasha was definitely attracted to Keir. Those beautiful, blue eyes of his and just the touch of his hand, made her want to tear his clothes off. She wasn't the type of girl who'd usually picture these kinds of things within milliseconds of meeting a man. In fact, in the two years she had been living in this beautiful city, Sasha had vowed to herself that men were off her radar. Sure, she had dated but she wasn't looking for anything serious.

Feeling as though time had stopped again, Sasha and Keir soon found themselves sipping their respective beverages and sitting with all the other people scattered about on the lawn. They found a prime spot, beside a towering eucalyptus tree toward the back of the crowd. For the next few hours, they'd make each other laugh. They'd share their respective stories, their likes and dislikes; all the things you'd expect from two people who had just connected. Oh, and Keir would tell Sasha that the photo was of his dead sister, a story that may sound half believable yet felt true to Sasha's ears.

From that day on, this is where the pair would meet for lunch, every single day for weeks. The chemistry between them was magnetic and it wasn't long until romance blossomed. It also wasn't long until the two had rendezvoused at almost every five-star hotel in the city. They carried on the 'handsome stranger' routine for months.

Her boyfriend had a kind demeanour despite his confident (yet reserved), 'Mr. social scene' type personality. You see, Keir was far from boring. He knew everybody that was anybody. He could be spontaneous, yet quiet; awkward, yet appropriate. Keir knew just how to be in every situation. He simply wasn't like anybody else that Sasha had ever met. As bright as his personality would shine and as suave as he could be behind closed doors, Keir knew how to dazzle Sasha. To Sasha, he was a movie star. He had those looks, that personality and was dripping with charm. He made her feel like his leading lady; his perfect match.

Keir was tall and always impeccably dressed. He resembled nothing of the boys Sasha used to know during her teens. He spoke so tenderly, and almost every time he opened his mouth, that abundance of butterflies would return to Sasha's stomach. He had his way with her. She was hooked.

A whirlwind romance it was, yet a passionate whirlwind at that. Keir was attentive and spoiled Sasha with beautiful dinners at fancy restaurants and weekends away at charming wineries, just a short drive from the city. There was a time when Sasha and Keir were inseparable. Her friends would question whether it was all too good to be true. From time to time, they would ask 'Sash, you sure he isn't married?' and to that she would irrefutably deny.

Keir was a gentleman and Sasha had no doubts. It was to be the beginning of their love story, or so she thought.

A few more months passed and Keir had been talking a lot about taking the next step. Sure, moving into Keir's apartment would have been a dream come true for Sasha as she loved her boyfriend and Keir adored her. The hospital where he worked as a surgeon was fairly close to his home near Pride Park, the setting of where they met a few short months before. It was a prime location and provided convenient walking access through the park to Sasha's workplace.

She absolutely cherished her job as an editor's assistant at Cruz Magazine. Cruz was a popular '20-something' publication for all things style, travel, health and love. Sasha adored her work – and she was good at it too.

To her detriment and perhaps down to her youth, Sasha rarely thought of tomorrow when it came to her relationship with Keir. Every other aspect of her life was faultlessly predictable. She was the kind of girl who had a plan for her plan, yet this new love was so spontaneous, she never once thought of tomorrow. This was all self-inflicted and on purpose. Sasha knew what she wanted from her career. She dreamt about lounging in the sun on the beaches of Santorini – when all her hard work would have paid off. In the future, she could envision having someone to share it all with, yet there was no rush. She was just so busy learning about herself like every other 20 something year old. Love, or anything pertaining to such a thing, was not yet a requirement in her already demanding life. Perhaps not until now. She had only just turned 20, and Keir, well he was older. Much older.

Keir and Sasha shared a courtship so fast that there was no time to contemplate - or ask why she hadn't already been invited to his apartment. Some nights when alone in her dainty studio, Sasha would imagine what the views were like from inside Keir's 13th floor apartment. It just seemed such a long way up from her little abode, set in a slightly rundown art deco building. Though Sasha was undeniably content. She loved her home in the city yet grew to adore Keir more. The realisation that this may very well be real, long lasting love came to her in a dream one evening, and when Keir asked her to move in, she simply thought, 'why not?' It wasn't to happen immediately, but that was okay with Sasha. She was hardly in any kind of hurry.

The loved-up pair were just so busy spending all their spare time in ultra-cool bars and restaurants which Sasha relished in. Keir sure treated his girlfriend like a lady, opening every car door and holding her hand as they strolled the city streets. Perhaps that was down to the age difference and maybe Keir was just 'old school'. Their age gap was vast, with Keir turning 36 in just a matter of months, but it didn't bother either of them one little bit.

Sasha could remember the very first time Keir had mentioned the concept of her moving into his apartment. It was over cocktails at 'Boire du vin'.

"The weather is shocking out there. You know darling, if you lived with me we could take a taxi home together" said Keir, in a deep and suggestive tone.

Sasha looked at him with 'yes please' written all over her blushing face.

"I will have to think about that mister" she replied, as she lent in close, teasing her man.

"Well let's make that happen soon, shall we?" said Keir, raising his glass to toast.

The pair were sitting side by side at a booth, totally loved up and blissfully happy. Not a person in sight wouldn't have noticed the older man and his younger lady.

'Judge away' Sasha thought to herself. She was purely intoxicated by Keir's charm that not one person could rain on her parade.

CHAPTER TWO

Bright Lights

With the steam clouding from my body, my breaths are shallow. I lay there, still; intoxicated by the candles that line my view, just above my painted toes. The tangerine tinged flames glisten as my body lay crimson from the heat. The silkiness of the warm, soap tainted water immerses me.

I am in heaven; I am in love.
My life is beautiful.

Always yours,

Rose

It was a rainy Friday night and Sasha was rushing to get ready for yet another epic date with Keir. They were meeting at the opening of 'Tuesday's Bar', a contemporary space downtown destined to become the hottest new establishment this year.

Dashing out through the door of her building with barely her heels on, Sasha caught a cab to meet Keir before making a fashionable entrance at Tuesday's. Despite the rain and the cold, she mimicked a movie star and was a total knockout.

As Sasha got out of the car, Keir simply couldn't take his eyes off her. From his girlfriend's perfect, red pout and alluring emerald eyes, right down to her long legs and designer shoes. Sasha knew she looked stunning and had the confidence to match. Keir appeared fetching himself, befitting to be standing next to Sasha in his midnight shade suit and tie.

They danced, they drank and then they danced some more. The dapper couple moved across the floor like a scene out of a black and white film. There was admiration by many who watched as Keir dipped Sasha, kissing her neck as she rose back up to stand. They were having the time of their lives. Finally retreating to a nearby table, Keir and Sasha took a break from the dance floor.

"This place is so beautiful!" announced Sasha, admiring the rich auburn colour of the panelled walls.

She darted her eyes around the room, admiring the sparkling ceiling and polished dance floor. For a few minutes, Sasha and Keir would play a game of 'spot the celebrity' which was a fairly easy game since the room was filled with them. Tuesday's opening night fell on the biggest television awards night of the year. People had come to celebrate their big wins, and others commiserated after working hard all year yet missing out against their industry peers. Many of these TV types craved recognition and it was easy to pick the winners from the losers. There was simply not a trace of humility in sight. People were just there to enjoy themselves and rightfully so. It was near impossible not to, Sasha thought. Tuesdays was like no place she had ever been, with its interior second floor balconies and a dance floor that went on and on. It was the most magical atmosphere, with lights bouncing across the room to the beat of the music.

"Honey, I'll be back in a moment" explained Sasha as she headed off toward the ladies' bathroom.

As Sasha stepped into a cubicle, she felt a vibration from her purse. It was late and very rare that a call would come through at that time of night. She quickly fumbled for her phone to answer the call.

"Hello?!" she shouted to overcome the echo of the music pumping in the next room.

It was her sister, Jess.

Sasha froze, not able to move.

She listened intently to Jess' words yet there she stood, motionless inside the tiny space. The loud music in the other room had hushed in Sasha's mind and all she could hear was the intense beat of her own heart. Her perfect pout turned to a stagnant frown and her emerald eyes, well they were just blankly glaring at the bronze tiled wall. As she stood there stunned, Sasha dropped her phone, the screen shattering due to the impact. The smash awakened Sasha, and it was like her whole world had been on pause for a moment. She quickly gathered as much of her phone as she could and retreated back to Keir. As she staggered toward him, her eyes welled up and Keir could tell that something was not right.

Whilst embracing his girlfriend, he desperately questioned her about what had happened.

"Did someone hurt you, darling? Are you okay?"

He sounded concerned and frantically stood up,

looking around the room for answers. Sasha began to open up and tell Keir about her call.

"It's my Mum. My Mum is…." she took a short breath in and out.

"She's gone Keir" explained Sasha as a waterfall of tears ran down her face.

She could barely set those words free.

Keir knew what that meant and instantly stood up straighter than before. What happened next was just plain bizarre. He seemed agitated before abruptly letting go of his love and without elucidation, walked out of the bar and onto the street. Shocked and purely confused, Sasha chased after him.

"Keir!" she called desperately.

"What are you doing?!"

"I can't deal with this. Just go! Get away from me!" screamed her boyfriend.

Unable to let anymore words out, Sasha stared frenziedly at Keir and wondered why he was acting so irrationally. She was the one who needed him, why did it seem like the tables had been turned?

Keir forcefully shoved Sasha as she tried to approach him, pushing her onto the damp, steel-cold footpath. He then proceeded to run frantically up the well-lit street, fleeing Sasha as if he was trying to escape.

Onlookers came to her aid, helping Sasha to her feet.

There she stood, dazed as she watched Keir in the distance deserting her. He had never been violent before, or this erratic.

'What is going on?!' she intrinsically thought.

Sasha kept still in the midst of the madness, clutching her sparkling shimmer purse. The rain continued to pour, drenching her soft blonde hair. Her cobalt blue gown was soaked all the way through. The cacophony of the bustling city street surrounding her was now partially muted by the patter of harsh raindrops hitting the rutted concrete.

People were rushing for protection from the downpour yet still, Sasha remained; standing there with the rain matching the tears that were plummeting from her eyes.

Her heart had been shattered. Her world had just crumbled; the usually vibrant and smiley Sasha was just numb.

The rainclouds then suddenly opened a little wider and let out a thunderous sound as the downpour started falling harder. Sasha felt the electricity just from the sound, rumble right through to the pit of her stomach. She suddenly felt awake from her reverie and scurried back to the nearby bar. As the rain eased, so did Sasha's tears. She soon hailed a cab and went home.

Stepping inside her tiny studio apartment, Sasha kicked off her heels and headed straight into her bathroom. As she struggled to tear off her soaking dress, Sasha's head was elsewhere.

'My mum, my beautiful mum!' she thought to

herself, desperately trying to reach for a reprieve; a break from the intense emotions that had taken her over.

Her mind kept wandering back to Keir and to how he had caused the most difficult moment of Sasha's life to date, to become even crueller; more crushing. There was just no explanation, nothing for Sasha. She had been left, totally deserted and with nobody to comfort her. He was gone and there wasn't anything she could have done to stop him.

Sasha turned on the shower, stripping down as the water heated up. Steam began to fill the room as she stepped inside. The goose bumps Sasha had caught from the cold night air began to diminish. Washing away that cool, drizzly night was the only reprieve Sasha could grasp onto. The warm water, running down her slender body, matched the trail of tears that trickled freely down both of her cheeks – just like the rain did only an hour before. Feeling raw and exposed to her emotions, Sasha's knees buckled and soon she found herself sitting on the shower floor. The sound of the water hitting the stark white tiles faded, as the only thing Sasha could hear was that heartbreaking phone call, playing over and over in her head.

'I just want my mum. Please! I'm not ready to lose her' thought Sasha in desperation.

'This is not happening. It is just not happening' she imagined, yet that just wasn't so.

As the water began to turn tepid, Sasha promptly stood up and turned the hot water tap on full, aiming to capture just a few more minutes. With the slightly warmer water running over her face, Sasha scrubbed away her makeup.

The rawness of what had happened would keep her awake almost all night.

CHAPTER THREE

The Day After

I want my Mum.

I just want my Mum.

No more words,

Rose

It was 7am as Sasha rolled over and faced the window. She had barely slept a wink. Slithers of light pierced through the blinds as Sasha felt around for her phone, shielding the morning sun with her forearm.

'No messages' she thought, as she tossed it next to where she was laying, tangled in her sheet on her ruffled bed.

Half expecting a call or text from her family, Sasha was a little disappointed. She was even more puzzled as to why she had not heard from the man who had supposedly loved her.

'What a joke that was' Sasha assumed, deeply hurt and feeling alone. It bothered her immensely that she hadn't heard from Keir. Surely, he had to know that running off like that was highly inappropriate. Her frustration was growing.

So, Sasha picked up her phone.

'Keir, I called you last night. Several times. Can you explain what happened? I'm a mess and I need to talk to you...'

Sending that text was all she could do, which was difficult especially since several deep cracks had wounded her phone. Thankfully Sasha had managed to piece it somewhat back together after dropping it the night before.

She had tried over and over to call him last night, yet each time her calls would go to voicemail; leaving Sasha no option but to leave blubbering messages as she tried to overcome her tears.

Sasha had never felt betrayal quite like the mountain of confusion and hurt that Keir had left her with. His behaviour was just so out of character.

'How could he be so cruel?' pondered Sasha.

'Why couldn't he see I needed him?'

These questions played over and over inside her already clouded head.

In the end, all Sasha knew was that she had to take stock of what had happened. There were plans to be made and Sasha knew that her family would need her around.

'It's time to go home' she thought as she sat up to get out of bed.

She picked up her phone and flicked through her contacts.

"I'll be buying the first ticket home, sis" she said speaking to her sister briefly.

"Please give dad a hug for me."

CHAPTER FOUR

Loose Ends

I cannot breathe. I cannot see... I cannot comprehend how things can get better. To have a mother as you were, how do I ever fill the gaping hole in my heart? How do I face the world knowing that I will never see you again? I am broken. I am lost. Where do I go from here? How do I reach down and pick up the pieces of my shattered spirit? How do I then place those pieces back together again when I know there's a piece that is forever lost?

How do I get through this?
I just don't know.

I will miss you forever,

Rose

❝You can do this... You can do this" whispered Sasha as she pulled her long, straight locks up into a messy bun.

Nodding her head and affirming her words, Sasha took a deep, drawn out breath before taking one last look at herself in her bathroom mirror.

As she walked out into her living room, it was a complete shambles. Boxes were everywhere as she'd been busy packing since returning from her mother's funeral only days before.

When Sasha was home on the family farm, she had

made the decision to quit her career and return to the country. She would always recall that very moment when her thoughts and feelings had aligned, revealing the answer; her answer to what should come next.

Home was where she felt she was needed. You see, Sasha couldn't imagine what her dad was going to do. He was aging, dealing with the passing of his beloved wife and he had to somehow learn to live on their large family property all his own. Sasha's father hadn't had to worry about being alone for almost thirty glorious years. Her mother was his rock, his soft place to fall.

She was simply the centre of his universe.

The funeral felt surreal to Sasha, almost like it was some kind of harrowing dream. Every face she'd pass were of people who knew her as the audacious little child she used to be. They shared their fond memories of Sasha and Jess growing up on the farm and with every conversation, Sasha felt that little bit more 'home' again.

During the service and as her mother's oak coffin was lowered into the ground, she anchored herself by holding the hand of her strong and stocky father. Her sister, Jess stood supportive on his other side, grasping her father's left hand. As the brown box lowered further, Sasha's legs shook. She felt herself giving in to the emotions that continued to try and beat her down. As she caught her very last glimpse of the wildflowers that laid across her mother's coffin, Sasha came to the revelation that there was no place like right here; beside her devastated father.

Nothing else mattered. Not her job, not her city lifestyle; nor any man for that matter. The comfort she felt from being home was much greater than all that put together.

The only thing left on Sasha's 'to do' list was to track Keir down and ask him one, simple question.

'Why?'

Slipping on her shoes and manoeuvring over the 'Leaning Tower of Pisa' of packing boxes piled up at her doorway, Sasha grabbed her purse.

She was sure that it wasn't going to be easy tracking down Keir. Sasha knew that if he wanted to speak with her he would have already done it. Ready for whatever may come with poise beaming from her emerald green eyes, she walked out into the hall with confidence; only to return minutes later to change out of the yoga pants she had chucked on in the morning.

Ready to face Keir, she re-entered the world beyond her apartment in 'oh so sexy' leather pants and killer red heels.

'I'm going to show him what he's missing!' she thought, channelling her mum who would have passionately told Sasha to tell him where to go. And if her daughter wasn't willing to shut this down on her own, Margaret would have happily hopped on the next bus to the city to do the deed on Sasha's behalf.

Arriving at the entrance of Keir's building, Sasha's heart was pumping. She had no idea how he was going to react, or if he would even see her.

Still, filled to the brim with self-assurance, she walked up and hit his apartment number.

And hit it again…

And again.

There was no response. He wasn't home and Sasha was far from satisfied. She needed this done. Sasha felt that if she was to return to the farm, she had to do it knowing that her slate was clean and no remnants of their broken relationship remained. The week just gone had been harrowing for Sasha and not having Keir by her side made her furious. Angry to the point that she ran into an open paddock on her parent's property and screamed at the top of her lungs. The release she felt wasn't parallel to anything she had ever felt before. Sasha was feeling ready to let this man go. Keir had discarded her in the most cruellest and confusing way. So here she was, standing in front of his building, peering up, looking around for any sign of Keir. Feeling nothing more than abandoned and dispensable; desperate and alone.

'If he had only called' thought Sasha, begging for an answer that would make sense.

Hitting the buzzer just more time, she was sure her efforts were for nothing.

"Coward!" she fervently said as she stepped away from the building.

Seconds later, a middle-aged woman dressed in the most elaborate canary coloured jumpsuit hit a bunch of numbers on the keypad and strolled ever so stylishly into Keir's building. Seeing an opportunity, Sasha sprinted toward the closing door, slipping off her stilts when she was just a step short. She had clumsily skun her knee on the terrazzo entrance of the stunning, formal atrium that greeted her as she began to peer up toward the ceiling. With the most ornate chandelier hanging flawlessly in the middle of the double height room, one could only imagine what was to come behind its golden walls.

"Ouch!" Sasha screeched, but ignored the damage to her knee and leather pants.

'I made it!' she thought to herself with relief, realising that her purse was wedged conveniently between the door and its frame. Climbing up to her feet, she retrieved her purse and without delay, pushed open the oversized glass door and quickly limped inside.

As the elevator opened on the 13th floor, Sasha again took one of her trademark deep breaths. She looked down and ever so carefully stepped out from the elevator into the extravagant hall. Gold seemed to be the theme and every surface shined like nothing she had ever seen before.

Nervous and emotionally vulnerable, Sasha bravely knocked on Keir's apartment door.

She waited a moment.

Then she knocked again.

For a minute, there was silence. The kind of quiet unresponsiveness that could drive a girl to her brink.

"Keir! Just answer the door. I really need to talk to you!" she called, losing her patience and trying to raise a reaction.

She turned her back to the door and put her head in her hands.

'He's not here' she thought to herself, feeling her eyes well up, giving into the grief. Sasha was shaking, her nerves causing her heart to pound; her head to feel heavy and sore. Cradling her forehead in her two hands, Sasha was finally defeated. There was nothing more that could be done. She'd called him, texted him numerous times, and even resorted to phoning the hospital where Keir worked. By this point, it was obvious to this heartbroken young woman. Keir was now just a memory, a once loved yet lost piece of her puzzle.

Moments later, Sasha heard the door to Keir's apartment. A slight murmur of sound coming from its hinges alerted her to turn back around.

Here was her moment.

To face the man who had caused all this confusion.

Except it wasn't him. It was a cleaner who had just finished servicing the apartment. The woman jumped back slightly, startled by the sight of Sasha's intense glare. She pulled out her earphones, ready to hear what Sasha had to say.

"Excuse me, I'm sorry to startle you. Would Keir Sterling be home at the moment?" Sasha asked, eagerly waiting for the response she craved.

The soft-spoken lady looked at Sasha with confusion. Perhaps because of the fright she had just experienced.

"There is no person by that name here. You must be confused with another apartment" she responded.

Sasha took a small step backward. She looked at the open door. Yes, the apartment number was correct. She recalled the floor number, ticking off this vital piece of information as well. Sasha was positive that Keir always talked about how magnificent the views were from the 13th floor; of the natural beauty of Pride Park, illuminated by the sky-scraping city lights.

None of this seemed to make any sense to Sasha. Lost in thought, she shook her head slightly, then noticed that the woman was still stagnantly standing there waiting for Sasha to speak.

"Oh, I'm sorry for holding you up" said Sasha, before retreating to the elevator.

As she exited the building, Sasha was leaving without her answers. She strolled out of the beautiful, ornate palace-like atrium with more questions than she had to begin with.

'He lied to me' she thought.

'He fucking lied to me.'

CHAPTER FIVE

Home

Silence; the one constant, is comforting,

yet all the while I think of him. My

limbs bind to the sounds of nothing,

motionless, yet full of life. Beads of water

trickle anonymously down my face.

Silent 'diamond like' drops run

aimlessly down my neck. The rest of my

body lay still, below the water's tip. I

have no time to wallow. He is gone and I

cannot wait for someone who could not

wait for me.

Reminiscent of wax softening, my body

continues to melt. My world is no longer the same. I miss my mother; her strength, her soft embrace and her fluorescent heart of gold. Like a flash, my eyes open! The sun that glistens so brightly blinds me and I raise my hand to shun from it. I turn my head, from left to right. 'Where am I?' I silently pondered, feeling the immense heat and wiping the sweat beads from my brow. 'I am home' I confirmed as I sunk deeply into the comfort of being back where I belong.

Grieving, yet still here,

Rose

Moving home to her family farm felt like the best decision Sasha could make after Keir and of course the death of her mother. She had quit her promising career in the city and traded it for a part-time receptionist role at a nearby local medical centre. This freed up time to help her father on the farm. Perhaps it wasn't what Sasha had hoped for, though her priorities had forcefully changed.

Sasha's father, Frank enjoyed her company as he took the passing of his beloved Margaret particularly hard. With Jess, soon to be leaving again to work interstate, Sasha was his one big comfort. He may not have told her often enough, but Frank enjoyed having

Sasha back home.

The day he lost his wife was by far the worst day of his life. Swerving to miss a kangaroo on quite a perilous bend, Margaret's car skidded off the road and into a big old gum tree. There was no way anybody could have survived the accident. Poor Margaret didn't have a chance. Frank was far from an angry man though like most farmers, he was a fixer and could make just about any piece of junk into something of value. By using that same kind of initiative, Frank was determined that no other motorist would meet a similar fate on that stretch of road. Without approval, he took it upon himself to saw down every tree close to that bend and just like that, no person would ever die on that road again.

Sasha's family came from miles around to grieve for her mother. She was well-loved and known for her tough exterior and soft, nurturing nature. Both Sasha and Jess spent a few weeks together with Frank, helping him with everything from farm work to cooking. It was almost like they were kids again, just with more responsibility and no mum to comfort them when life felt lonely.

Although they lived a fair distance from each other, Sasha and her sister, Jess were quite close and that bond became the most evident each time they would come together. Jess had a quick wit and could fool Sasha in any situation. Once she convinced her younger sister who was 5 at the time that their dad was growing babies in his vegetable garden and that when the next one was ready to be picked, Sasha was going to be given away to another family to make room for the brand-new vegetable garden bub. Was Sasha just gullible? Perhaps. An avid day dreamer? Absolutely! And sometimes that imagination of hers would grow a mind of its own.

Jess was quite the joker, even for her then, 8 years. Perhaps that could have been the reason she became a stand-up comedian, doing gigs all around the country. Her mild success didn't pay all the bills, yet it certainly gave her a cult-like following on social media. Jess was determined to make it work and gave most of her time to building up her comedic brand.

"Hey Sash, pass me the tea towel" asked Jess who was about to pull a steaming hot roast chicken out of the oven. That was her other talent. Jess didn't just know how to make a crowd cackle, she could also cook! And cook very well indeed. When Jess wasn't travelling the countryside and headlining gigs, she would pick up casual chef work wherever she could, mostly in pubs dotted around Australia. All the money she was making helped finance her impressive nomad lifestyle.

Tossing the tea towel Jess' way, Sasha kept thinking of how happy she was to be at home with her sister. They didn't have a whole lot in common yet still somehow, they clicked. Jess was a ball of energy, sports mad and adventurous. Sasha was dedicated to staying grounded and a little more refined than her audacious sister. They were much more similar when growing up, yet something changed and Sasha took a different route; choosing city life and all the trimmings. There was zero chance of Sasha jumping out of planes and conquering mountains although Jess lived for all that kind of caper. Sasha would much rather spend her weekends sipping a mocha whilst reading a glossy magazine or, watching a good movie. Anything that didn't involve risk to one's life was okay by Sasha.

"I need to talk to you about something Sash" announced Jess as she placed the scorching hot tray onto the top of the old range.

"Sure. What's on your mind?" responded Sasha, inquisitively.

Jess appeared nervous. She was biting half of her bottom lip like she'd always do in difficult situations.

"Do you think Dad would be cool if I brought somebody to meet you guys? Perhaps next time I come home?" asked Jess.

Sasha cheekily grinned.

'Oh, is that all?' she thought, before speaking her answer.

"Awe! My big sister has a boyfriend!" she teased, playfully taunting Jess.

"Who is he? What's his name?"

Jess looked at her sister, appearing more nervous than ever. She bit her lip again, this time a little tighter and paused. This apprehension wasn't a usual trait of Jess who'd usually just blurt anything out and Sasha caught on quickly that something wasn't quite right here.

"So, are you going to spill?"

As Jess continued to serve dinner that is exactly what she did.

"I have met somebody but there's one thing wrong with what you just said" she apprehensively responded.

"He is actually a 'she' Sash" explained her sister, "I'm dating a woman."

At that very moment Sasha could almost feel her jaw hit the floor. She did not see this coming.

"I don't expect you to say anything Sash. I just wanted to tell you what was going on" continued Jess, with some relief written all over her face.

Sasha wasn't for one moment bothered with the fact that her sister was seeing a woman. Yet for some reason she handled the entire situation wrong. Instead of trying to assure Jess that she was happy for her, Sasha didn't say a word, opting for silence, followed by barely there conversation about unrelated things.

That night after dinner they went to bed early. When all was quiet and all Sasha could hear was the sound of the crickets chirping outside, she reflected on what Jess had said and just how pathetic her response was.

'I should have hugged her. Instead I left her thinking that I couldn't care less' she thought.

Sasha feared worse than that. She considered herself far from homophobic.

'What if she thinks I don't approve? I am such an idiot!'

Instead of sleeping, Sasha tossed and turned feeling

like a fool, until she heard a delicate tap on her bedroom door.

"Yes? Come in" said Sasha, when she realised who it was.

Peering around the door was Jess.

"Hey" she said quietly, "is it cool if I come in?"

Sasha nodded.

"Of course, you can. Sit down" she said, propping herself up and patting a spot on the bed just below her feet. The light of the full moon shining through the window added a glow to Jess' face.

Jess sat down and immediately began to speak.

"I want you to know…"

Sasha cut her off, placing her palm on top of Jess' trembling hand.

"If this is about earlier, I'm sorry. I just had no idea!"

Jess looked up to the ceiling for a moment, as if she was gathering her thoughts. She then stared right at her sister who was anxiously waiting for what was to come.

"I thought out of everyone you would be the safest person to tell" expressed Jess.

"Honestly, you were the one person I thought who would support me. I'm sorry if it shocked you Sash but, this is who I am."

Sasha could see the relief that was written all over Jess' face.

Forever the over-thinker, this left Sasha feeling sad,

and quite disappointed in herself. It was clear at that very moment, that her life with Keir in the city had consumed her. Perhaps, thought Sasha, if she hadn't been so wrapped up in him and all the trappings of his world, perhaps; just perhaps, she would have been available to Jess.

Sasha tried hard to fight the thoughts that kept flooding in. Memories of when she didn't come home for her mother's last birthday and how she had only spoken to Jess on the phone twice in the past few months. The time she spent with Keir now seemed like a superficial waste of her time.

'Family first' she thought, as she hugged her sister, giving her the most loving, overdue embrace.

"I feel sick that you see me like this Jess."
Sasha said, speaking directly from her heart.

"I love that you are you, and that you are honest and true to who you are. I want to know everything about you Jess. I totally support everything you do, and everything you are. You will never receive judgement from me. Not intentionally, ever, ever again."

Sasha barely took a breath and placed her hand on her chest.

"I'm sorry that I gave you the impression that I didn't care. I do. I really do. I wholeheartedly do and I will support you in talking to Dad whenever you're ready. And this lady in your life? Well she is family to me now. I want you to know that."

Her rambling declaration put the most relieved, and full smile on Jess' face. Sasha could see that this unconditional sisterly love was all that Jess had been craving.

"Thanks Sash. I don't know how dad will take it but I'm so glad you are accepting. I kind of knew you would be."

Sasha smiled back and held her sister's hand tight.

"You know, mum would have been happy for you" she said, softly.

"Dad will be too."

Jess shook her head.

"I doubt it Sash. He won't be expecting it and you know what he's like."

Through simply clasping her sister's hand, Sasha could sense her nervousness. This wasn't easy for Jess despite her usual attitude toward most things. Her sexuality was immensely personal and not something Jess would want to put a microscope on.

"Be positive!" Sasha advised her sister.

Perhaps a little naïve, but hopeful for the journey ahead.

"Dad will process it and soon we'll be welcoming you back here with your lady. So, tell me all about her... Don't stop at her name. I want to know everything!"

Sasha was so pleased to be developing a new layer to her relationship with Jess. They barely ever talked about romantic relationships or things of that nature and Sasha felt that it was time she made up for the past few months of little contact.

So that set Jess off. She told Sasha all about Ally and how happy she was. Finally, Sasha had been given the opportunity to truly know her sister, as Jess unlocked her world and invited her sister in.

"Jess, let's forge ahead with no secrets" she declared, with a playful grin on her face. They sealed it with a 'pinkie promise' and hugged one more time.

"Oh, and I'll try to tell dad. Before I leave on Friday" added Jess, sounding a little less apprehensive than before.

Sasha smiled.

"Sis, it'll be okay."

The next morning, Sasha was sitting at the dining table, eating cereal and flicking through the latest copy of Cruz Magazine. Last night's conversation was still on her mind although the regret she was feeling had taken centre stage in her mind. Sasha had not seen her mother for months before she was tragically killed. Instead, she chose to spend months being wined and dined by a man she barely knew over precious time with her family. Living with this put a knot in the pit of Sasha's stomach. She labelled herself a fool for falling into such a trap and vowed never to make that same mistake again. But it was too late. Her mother was gone and Sasha would never have the opportunity to tell her how she felt; a deep, mutual love that could not be replicated. By this point, the contents of her old favourite magazine had become a blur and Sasha was just sitting there, lost among her own self-sabotaging thoughts.

Awoken from her momentary daydream, she was roused by the sound of Jess entering the kitchen.

"Sash, I think now is a better time than any" said Jess, gazing out the back window. She opened the curtain a little wider, so Sasha could see. There was Frank, at his most relaxed. Picking tomatoes for the mother of all batches of Margaret's famous sauce.

"I'll call him inside" said Sasha, walking up behind Jess and placing her hand on her sister's shoulder, offering some much-needed support.

"Dad! Can you come in for a minute please?" called Sasha, and Frank look up, following the sound of his daughter's voice.

It wasn't long until Frank appeared, shuffling in through the back door. He took one look at his daughters and sat down, placing his old hat on the round wooden table. Jess took a seat opposite him. Sasha could feel Jess' intense nerves almost telepathically, just by reading the expression on her face. She looked on, at her father and at her sister; hoping, praying, wishing that this conversation would play out the way she desperately wanted it to. The truth was, Sasha didn't know how it would go and by the look of Frank's face, he wouldn't have seen this coming.

"Okay girls, what's this all about?" he said, gruffly, yet with a slight grin on his face. This was typical for Frank; stern yet jolly. Tough yet fair.

Jess looked at her father and began to tell him about Ally. His face gave nothing away. One could have cut the tension in the room with a knife as this stagnant moment in time, blanketed the room with silence. Frank showed not one ounce of emotion toward Jess. He had nothing but a blank stare, directed at the rustic wooden boards that covered the kitchen floor. His silence led Sasha into thinking that this was going to end badly and that Jess may have been right in her earlier prediction. Perhaps he wouldn't accept it, perhaps he could not understand. The room was so quiet that a mouse scurrying across the floor could have been heard. In a bid to end the awkwardness, Sasha spoke up.

"Dad?" she interrupted.

"Are you alright? What are you thinking?"

Frank was still; and fairly expressionless.

"I have nothing to say on the matter."

His words were ice cold. Neither of his daughters could have predicted this kind of response from Frank. Leaning his large, worker hands flat on the table in front, Frank used it to steady himself as he rose to stand.

"Dad!" said Sasha as she spied Jess slumping down in her chair.

"You can't be serious!"

With total confusion written all over her face, Sasha stood up as well and attempted to look her father in the eye.

"Look at me dad!" she said, trying to rouse him from

his thoughts.

Though Frank would not budge and took the opportunity to walk out the back door, leaving both of his daughters in disbelief. By this time, Jess had begun to rest her face in her hands and Sasha could see how devastated she was.

She could see that her sister was beginning to breakdown, as tears began to try and escape the strong clasp Jess had covering her eyes. Sasha was desperate to take her sister's sorrow away.

"I'm just disappointed, that's all" said Jess, choking back her tears.

"I don't know why I expected anything more."

As she began to let go, Jess rose from her chair and hurried out of the room, leaving Sasha to make a decision. Taking a ginormous breath, Sasha listened to her heart.

She bolted toward the back door. Deep inside she knew that Jess needed her most though here was her moment to make a difference. As the door slammed behind her, she peered out into the garden where she saw Frank, closing the vegetable patch gate behind him. Instead of calling out and making a scene, Sasha decided to calmly approach him. As she walked through the slightly unkempt open lawn toward her father, Sasha took another deep breath; her heart pounding fast in anticipation for this moment.

'This is going to be one difficult conversation…' said

the little voice inside her head.

As she reached the old, rickety gate, Sasha placed both her arms on the top rail, resting them there. She looked at Frank who had his back turned; his body slightly slouched tending to his tomatoes.

"With all due respect, that wasn't fair Dad" said Sasha, bravely going straight to the point.

As she spoke, she saw Frank shuffle on over to the next plant.

"I don't get why you're so silent over this. Jess being gay doesn't change anything. Why make this a thing?"

Frank remained silent for a good minute before turning his head towards Sasha. He was staunch, and his expression told the story.

"Go inside" he responded, in a brusque tone.

Sasha saw red. Her eyes widened as she opened the gate and marched on through. She had never stood up to her father quite like this before.

"No! Dad, I will not go inside! You need to see what this is doing to Jess" she explained with confidence, "now go undo the damage you've caused!"

Sasha stood her ground, steadfastly staring her father in the eye. As he looked back, Sasha knew her efforts were likely to be for nothing. He wasn't about to budge. From that moment, Sasha knew that Jess being gay was a deal breaker for Frank. Yet still, no part of her could understand why.

'Because there simply was no good reason why' said

the little voice inside her head, again stating the unfair truth.

Feeling as though she was beating a dead horse, Sasha made her way back inside to find her sister. And she found her. Sitting silently in the living room, her knees crunched up toward her chest.

"I know, it didn't go well" said Sasha, stating the obvious.

"Maybe give it a day or so. He'll come around."

Jess shook her head.

"No. We are done here" said Jess, with a strange sense of surety.

Sasha turned her head, puzzled by this. In her mind, this was far from over and Frank accepting Jess was not negotiable.

"Why do you say that?"

Jess looked up at her sister.

"Because I'm terrified Sash" she said, her voice shaking as the words flowed out.

"I might not ever come back to the farm again."

Sasha was sure that it would never come to this and wanted to make Jess see that her dad wouldn't ever abandon her.

"He will come around. You just wait and see."

Jess definitively shook her head and her facial expression switched from disappointment to a tenacious glare. Sasha saw what felt like an instant wall erect in front of Jess.

"No, Sasha. If he doesn't accept all of me, I'm done" she explained.

"He either accepts all of me or none of me. It's his choice."

Sasha's heart sank and she could not come up with a response to that. It was a fair statement, she thought. In her heart, Sasha saw why Jess felt this way. In her head, she could envision her family falling further apart.

The very next day, Jess was gone. Sasha begged her to stay but to no prevail and was devastated when she was left; alone on the farm with Frank.

A day or two passed and the pair were still not talking a whole lot. This suited Sasha in some ways as she had nothing positive to say to her father. He had not only let down Jess. Sasha was feeling the pain too. Saying goodbye to Jess felt eerily similar to losing their mother all over again; and to make things worse, Sasha had developed this disconnect from her father. A man she always felt that she could rely on. She begged herself to understand him though she couldn't. The whole situation felt like madness inside Sasha's head. None of it made sense and she could not escape the realisation that Jess was never coming home. It all just seemed like nothing would ever be the same again.

CHAPTER SIX

Goodbye, Sister

They say home is where the heart is

Well that is far from true,
For this old house is empty
All because of you.

I wish you knew the pain you caused
When you sent her on her way,
You broke her heart into pieces
You should have made her stay.

So here we are alone
In this creaky, beaten shell,
Silently just existing
In your self-inflicted hell.

Rose

There were days when all she wanted to do was run away. Then nights where the guilt would set in, and she'd spend time pondering about what her mother would say.

'None of this would have happened if mum was here.'

Sasha would recite these words to herself regularly, trying to explain away the bomb that had just gone off in her family. Her attempts may have been unsuccessful and perhaps a little irrational, though she longed for her mother. Sasha knew that her mum would have had the power to bring her family back together. She also knew that perhaps that baton had just been passed onto her.

Fixing her broken family was far from easy. Jess had stopped answering Sasha's calls and completely cut herself off from everybody. Again, Sasha felt abandoned.

First her mother.

Then Keir.

Now her sister.

So even though in her heart she felt that Frank was wrong, he was all Sasha had. And in time, their relationship improved and began to return to a new kind of normal; sombre yet better than it was.

Frank was one busy man, despite Sasha being around to help out whenever she could. As time passed, the wounds of Jess leaving healed little by little. Frank and Sasha began to communicate better although still, they lived slightly separate lives despite living under the one roof. As her hours increased at the clinic in town, Sasha had to spend more time away from the farm, and this led Frank into making a decision. With great apprehension, he was forced to employ somebody to take care of the day to day operations of his property. This was incredibly difficult for Frank as he didn't like change. Fortunately, it took just a short time for Frank to fill the position, arranging for a young family to move into the little white house on the hill. The family were to be arriving today yet Frank had neglected to tell Sasha. He was sometimes forgetful and with their relationship the way it was, the fact that Sasha didn't know was no surprise to her.

It had been a slow morning for Sasha. She got up late and was still in her singlet and pyjama shorts when there was a sharp tap on the old wooden screen door.

"Anybody home?"

Sasha sat upright on the sofa. She knew that voice! Quickly, Sasha off the couch and around to the door, trying to flatten her bed hair with her two open hands.

There stood a familiar face, a blast from the past of sorts.

"James! It's been so long!" she said as she gasped with excitement when opening the door. The tall and very good-looking young man that stood before her grinned and showed just as much surprise.

"Hi Sash, it sure has been a long time" he replied, with a smile, "I heard along the grapevine you were living back home."

There he was. Her childhood sweetheart staring back at her. Wearing a grey t-shirt that fit firmly around his arms, dusty jeans and the most glorious, wholehearted country smile.

Sasha went to hug James when suddenly, behind him appeared a woman holding a small baby. Awkwardly and somewhat abruptly, Sasha stepped back to capture a better view. James had become three; a family of three.

The Lawler's came from another farm close by and were looking for a new start when they were offered the opportunity to manage 'Maggie Creek', aptly named after his beloved. James, the son of a farmer, his wife, Claire and baby son, Dylan were to move into the little white cottage just at the top of the hill. James was an old school friend of Sasha's so the families knew each other well. In fact, James was her high school flame and the relationship ended when Sasha relocated to the city for work. It wasn't too serious and no hearts were broken. Although they missed each other's company for many months as any young lovebirds would.

From that day on, and after a quick chat, James, Claire and Dylan took the keys to their new cottage and settled in.

Sasha was quietly impressed at how well the family fitted in on Maggie Creek. James quickly proved to Frank that he was a hard worker. He worked tirelessly as all farmers do to ensure the property didn't fail whilst Frank struggled with the passing of his wife. As time passed, James would become the son that Frank never had.

Sasha was so pleased that some of the pressure had been eased off her father who said for as long as he was around, no one else would be running his place. Thankfully, common sense prevailed and Frank realised how much he really did need some time off from the monotony of every day farming life. He had casual helpers that would come and go although Frank never considered a permanent employee for his land. When James started working on the farm, Frank even took a short trip to visit Aunt Norma who lived in a small town at the top of Australia. He never liked leaving the farm so Sasha knew he had to be struggling. Although he didn't express it well, Sasha felt that he needed to escape all reminders of the love he had just lost. With James' commitment to the farm and Sasha there holding the fort as well, Frank was able to let go and that was just what he needed; a chance to begin moving on.

Life was sure a lot simpler on the family farm for Sasha, although she tired easily of country life in the beginning, especially when the weekends came around. There were no more swanky parties or fine dining, just the usual pub meals at the local a few k's down the road.

"Dad? What do you think about going for a meal tonight?" Sasha would ask but her father often declined, citing he had too much work to do in the very impressive vegetable garden, his other passion second to his farm work.

There were only a handful of times where he would respond with a hesitant 'yes'. Overall, Sasha felt lonely but soon she would strike up a friendship with the housewife on the hill, Claire.

Claire and Sasha were only a year apart in age. They didn't have a lot in common except their country upbringings however, somehow, they just clicked. Reminiscent of Sasha's relationship with Jess. Claire was veracious, very out-spoken and never had the conundrum of not being able to speak her mind. Yet first and foremost, Claire was a loving mother to Dylan who was only a few months old when the family moved to Maggie Creek. From that very first day standing at the door of her father's farmhouse, Sasha desperately wanted to feel nothing but jealousy over Claire though as time went on, she couldn't help but like her.

It was an odd pairing given Sasha and James' past romance but that didn't seem to matter. Sometimes, during her loneliest moments, Sasha would imagine what life may have been like if she had stayed on the farm. Would she have been just another version of Claire?

Being the only women on the property, Sasha and Claire became quite close. They would often journey to town together with Dylan and do the shopping for both households. The pair would sometimes take the baby for walks in his stroller and browse the few shops dotted about town. Sometimes Claire would even meet Sasha after work for dinner at the pub. It sure was a sombre life but Sasha soon began to enjoy her new (yet old) surroundings. No taxis, no trams and no real schedule. Life was beginning to feel normal for her again and Keir couldn't be further from her mind.

CHAPTER SEVEN

utterly charmed by you

You know that feeling when something feels so right, but so wrong at the same time? I experience it in moments of weakness, days where I feel impulsive... Times when you are the only one who plays on my mind. You have this way of gaining my attention and I fail to find the words to explain how. If I can never be with you, I can still dream...

Every word is meaningful
Gentle in its touch,
Words so very mesmerizing
I pine for them so much.
You hold me ever so gently
Moving closer; I feel you breathe,
Mesmerizing with your eyes

Your presence makes me weak.
With every whispered word, you speak
Accompanied by eyes so blue,
I hang by every letter
Paused; utterly charmed by you.

So, you see my sweet, I love you! Why
can't I tell you this out loud? Why can't
my dreams come into fruition? One day
I'll meet someone like you and I will no
longer spend my days daydreaming of
my lost love. I love you J.

Yours (in my dreams),

Rose

The blinding sun shined harshly onto the windscreen, as Claire drove down the rough, unsealed driveway. Early one morning, Sasha, Claire and little Dylan were headed to town again for another bout of grocery shopping and perhaps a good coffee; the only activity that reminded Sasha of her previous life.

"Wow, this sun is annoying Sash! I wish I'd brought my sunglasses" Claire complained as she drove through the farm gates.

"I know what you mean. It's brutal!" Sasha responded, equally bothered by the piercing yellow glow from the sky.

"I'm getting a headache already!" whined Claire, "luckily the drive is short."

About halfway to town along the quiet, country road, they suddenly heard a loud 'POP!'

"Bloody hell! There goes a tyre!" exclaimed Claire, whilst pulling to the side of the road.

She was right, they'd hit something on the road and it had caused one of the tyres to burst. With no coverage on their phones, the three had to flag a passing car for assistance. Not many vehicles frequented this long stretch of road though luckily Ted Murray, one of Frank's good mates soon stopped to lend a hand. He said he'd happily change the tyre so that they could keep on their journey to town, only to realise there was no actual spare in the boot. Instead, Ted stopped by Maggie Creek as the property was not far out of his way. A short time passed and James came along with a new tyre and tools to complete the job.

"I take it that it hasn't been a good morning for you two" he said stating the obvious, as he walked over carrying a tyre on one arm and tools in the other.

As James began to raise the car with a jack and unbolt the tyre, Sasha couldn't help but notice him. He had grown into a very attractive man, a little scruffy but that didn't bother her at all. He had a real and striking presence, and she could stare at him all day.

'That smile' she thought, as she watched on, despite the fact that his wife stood beside her, swaying as she rocked their baby son.

James' toned and tanned arms were on display through his firm grey t-shirt. His hair; short, dark and a little messy. Sasha would often catch herself spending moments peering over at James doing chores around the farm. He was so hardworking and there was just something about his rugged look that turned her on. Never had she found herself lingering for so long. Soon, she gave herself an 'imaginary slap in the face' and urged herself to quit staring.

'There's no way he'd be ever interested in me now. He's a married man!' Sasha thought to herself.

She felt ridiculous even having those sorts of feelings enter her head.

Once the tyre was replaced, James watched Claire start the car and re-commence the voyage into town. He then turned his vehicle around and drove off in the opposite direction back toward Maggie Creek.

After shopping all morning (and spending an hour sipping latte's and nattering at the local bakehouse), Sasha, Claire and Dylan returned home. They were greeted by Frank and James enjoying a beer on the front veranda of the farmhouse at midday.

"It's too early for that isn't James?!" snapped Claire.

James moaned in response to his wife, giving her an objectionable look. Often blunt and not one to mince his words, Frank sniped back at Claire.

"He's a hard worker Claire. Nothin' wrong with a beer or two after a mornin' of hard yakka. I'm giving him the arvo off!"

Claire stomped off in a huff and returned home to the cottage, leaving Sasha to grab her own cold beer and join the men.

"Frank, I've gotta say, living and working on Maggie Creek has been great, and sorry about Claire, she's just had one of those days" explained James, trying to smooth things over.

Frank looked up at him and replied swiftly.

"It's alright mate. I think you're doin' a top job and we like havin' you around, don't we darl?"

Frank turned to look at his daughter for acknowledgement.

"Yeah Dad, you've been a huge help J, we really appreciate it" responded Sasha, with a nod.

'J' was what she affectionately nicknamed James back when they were at school.

"Anyway! On that note, I might go check the patch for some new developments!" said Frank in a merry manner, as his weathered hands pushed on the sides of his chair, raising him slowly from the old recliner.

His chair was as rough as it could be yet with a blanket strewn over it, the relic was good enough for Frank. So off he shuffled out the back to tend to his vegetables, leaving James and Sasha to continue without him.

Looking over at each other and sharing a short giggle over Frank's jovial exit, the pair continued to chat. They re-lived the old days and talked candidly about the new ones. Sasha confided in her old friend about her anomalous experience with the man she thought she'd marry and James opened up about his troubled marriage, citing that he just wasn't happy anymore. Neither of them imagined that they would ever have a moment to talk again as not so long ago, it would have been geographically unlikely that they'd ever cross paths again. Four short hours passed by and it was time to settle in for the night. James returned up the hill and Sasha went inside to prepare dinner.

Days went by and all Sasha could think about was 'what could have been'. If she had stayed, would she be in Claire's position? She visualised how life could have been, perched up on top of the hill, calling the little cottage 'home' with James. She imagined greeting him at their door and spending long, cool nights cuddled up by the fireplace, watching television or talking away just like they did a few short nights ago. Sasha pictured waking up beside her love, watching him edge closer to kiss her forehead before going off to work each day on the farm. Her heart would not let her forget her feelings for James, no matter how much she tried.

Sasha's attraction to her old flame remained silent, yet their connection lingered. He seemingly felt the same way though Sasha couldn't be positive because discussing such feelings was totally off the table. What began as a joke and playful banter among friends, began to mean something else. She felt it; it seemed they both felt it.

CHAPTER EIGHT

The Hot Tin Shed

My mind boggles as to how I got myself into this. I want to spend time with him yet how do I ensure no lines are crossed? I simply cannot. My innate desire to be with J is just too intense right now and to stay apart is tearing ME apart. Dad is doing better so maybe I should go back to the city where I know I could stay out of trouble!

No! I just need to confront this and end it once and for all.

I'll go back to the city after I talk to J. I must stop feeling this way.

Forever the bridesmaid,
Rose

Whispering sweet words to James became more regular, more impulsive. He wanted more and she wanted more; although they knew pursuing anything would be dangerous ground. Sasha's feelings for the farm hand could not reach any higher peak. She was in love with him and it was clear he felt the same the way.

Late one night, at about 9pm, James was busy in the shed replacing a part on the old, beaten four-wheeler. All he wanted to do was go home and crack a beer after a long day sowing wheat, yet he persevered as any hardworking farmer would. It was a sweltering night and with sweat beading on his forehead he took off his singlet and wiped his brow. With his shirt draped over his shoulder, he put his head back down and continued the job.

Moments passed and in the dark of the night, James suddenly heard someone approaching the shed. He instantly popped his head up and peered toward the open roller door. The light from a torch darting in the distance was all he could see and he couldn't make out who was approaching. The shed was situated down off the hill and only a minute's stride from the main house. 'It can't be Claire?' thought James as if it was his wife, she would have driven down. Frank wouldn't venture out this late at night as he would have been in a deep slumber by now. All that could usually be heard from the shed at this time was the rustling of the wind as it collided with the old tin walls, along with crickets piping their familiar sound. So, James wasn't expecting anyone to be out and about.

As he began to realise who it was, a soft whisper came from the darkness.

"Hey J, what are you doing out here at this time of night?"

His visitor was Sasha.

Looking puzzled, James responded.

"I could ask you the same question myself!"

Sasha chuckled, switching her torch off as she stepped into the lit shed.

"Well I was still up and I saw your light on. I guess I just figured we need to talk and this could be our opportunity" she said, nervously awaiting a reply.

James awkwardly placed his hands on the back of his head and turned to face the back wall. His actions, although quiet, spoke a thousand words. After a big breath and a few seconds later, he turned back around to face Sasha. With a look one only could describe as restrained, James began to talk.

"Sash, you know this is awkward and bad timing… And, and all of that. It's not right but I can't not say this". He continued, "I need some time. You know things aren't good with me and Cl…"

"I want to stop you right there!" Sasha rebutted abruptly forcing a full stop to James' sentence.

"I just can't sit around waiting for you!" explained Sasha to James.

"You can't just lay this on me and expect some kind of… Some kind of subdued reaction!"

James' eyes dropped to his feet, his hands remain clasped behind his head. He began to pace with no real direction.

"Well I don't know what to say Sasha! I have a wife and a son. I can't just go up and tell 'em I'm leavin' right now! And what about your dad? Have you forgotten that he's my boss?!" said James, as a surge of frustration leaked to the surface of his mind.

Sasha looked at him with disbelief, yet couldn't help noticing the sweat beading on his shirtless body. She knew she'd never be able to wait for James however, clearly Sasha had a strong attraction to him.

"I…" she paused, as a plethora of thoughts entered her mind. If she was ever going to speak her mind to James, this was the moment. This was her opportunity to finally burst and tell James just how she felt.

"I get it okay! I understand we shouldn't even be feeling this way let alone discussing it. I know there's so much at stake. But I… I want you J. I think about you all the time and I shouldn't, and I know it's not right" rambled Sasha, trying to scramble for words that made sense.

"Simply put, I just feel we're supposed to be or something. I can't tell you how or why I know that. There's just something about you".

James, a little more at ease now had calmed down. He felt an instant correlation with what Sasha was saying.

"I feel the same way" he responded looking up and peering into Sasha's deep jasmine eyes. James took a step toward Sasha, with a frivolous anticipation for something more. The tension in that moment soon became too much for the two of them to bare. Sasha pounced on James and kissed him passionately in a fervent embrace. With his warm breath on her neck and her soft lips on his, they pressed up against the wall, leaving a dent in the tin. Their connection was unmeasurable, with every touch, their passion heightened until soon they were making love. With Sasha's legs wrapped around James' body and her tight, denim skirt scrunched up around her hips, they stared into each other's eyes; knowing, hoping, believing that, they were only doing what they should have done long ago. Their craving for each other was finally being met and soon it was all over.

They didn't feel quite so good anymore.

As James rustled to pick up his trousers, Sasha looked away as her desire for James began to transform into shame. Silently, the two parted ways with Sasha returning home. James slept in the shed that night, unable to face his wife. The allure he felt for Sasha was still there and he could not have looked Claire in the eye. The ignominy was just too great and to kiss his son goodnight - as James would each time he'd return home... Well, that was just a thought too much.

CHAPTER NINE

The Aftermath

GUILT. It'll shake you 'til you're on your knees, And have you begging, 'please, oh please.'

GUILT. Makes you the gatekeeper of the pain, And screams at you that you're to blame.

GUILT. It won't let you rest until you know, The kind of hurt that you bestow.

GUILT. It will rip at you until you're raw, And leave you shaken to your core.

GUILT. It won't rest until you've seen, The kind of bitch that you have been.

Denial. I choose denial.

In love yet utterly foolish,

Rose

The following day as she woke, Sasha was still plagued by what had occurred that crimson summer night. Here lay a torn young woman, alone; feeling a range of self-centred and raw, mixed emotions. On one hand, Sasha felt assured. James had made it clear that he wanted her as much as she wanted him. Sasha had craved his affection for so long that regardless of James' marriage, she couldn't help but immerse herself in the fantasy. On the other hand, she felt scorn, like a complete and utter fool. She knew that James wasn't the kind of guy to leave his responsibilities behind for anybody. Yet he was the kind of man to cheat, and this played on Sasha's mind. She pondered whether this really meant something to him.

'Would he ever leave Claire?' she wondered. These dangerous thoughts continued to flood her head. What plagued Sasha the most was, no matter how wrong it was, it still felt right. An empathy-free kind of justification for an act that in reality could never be seen as okay.

By this time, she had pulled her hair up into a messy ponytail and began to make her way out to the farmhouse kitchen. The sound of her footprints hitting the old floorboards as she walked down the hall echoed her mood; sombre and just holding it together. For this wasn't like anything Sasha had experienced before. Her brain wouldn't let her rest. James couldn't leave her thoughts for more than a second. She had this moral conflict in her mind that wouldn't be resolved quickly. Sasha knew this, and wished things could be simpler.

It wasn't long until she began to think about James' son again, like she had one hundred times before during the past eight hours. She knew that meddling with the fragility of a family wasn't right and the feelings she was developing in the pit of her stomach confirmed this. Then the insults started.

"You're such an idiot!" said Sasha under her breath. She didn't stop there, and let her debilitating comments beat her down until a lone tear streamed down her face. Sasha shook her head, before pulling the bread back out of the toaster. Suddenly she realised that there was no way this all would end well. It became blatantly obvious to Sasha that she and James were history, and history they should have stayed.

'There's no time for breakfast' she thought, placing the slices in the bin nearby. She couldn't have stomached them anyway. Even though by this time Sasha has begun to see just how foolish she'd been, nothing could stop her from lusting after this man. So, to avoid the inevitable wave goodbye or morning walk with Claire, she left early for work that day, determined not to look any of the Lawler family in the eye.

The day was to bring a cool change, which was a welcome reprieve to all on Maggie Creek and surrounds. It had been a particularly dry summer, every farmers nemesis. Arriving at work, she was greeted by the doctor's wife who announced that she was off to an appointment out of town. This meant Sasha was flying solo today. The office was petite, and serviced the small town comfortably. Dr Stone had spent most of his career here and even lived onsite in a renovated weatherboard house attached to the clinic.

"It's a lovely morning isn't Sasha?" he said as he placed a pile of magazines on her desk.

"We were donated these for the patients. Please refresh the supply when you have a moment."

"Sure Doctor" Sasha responded, with a smile, seemingly pushing back the moral fist fight that was going on in her head.

Dr Stone peered over Sasha's shoulder. She was waiting for the computer to load, ready for the first patient.

"Who is first on our list?" he asked.

"We have…" she paused, as the program loaded.

"We have Mrs. Simeoni up first today."

Dr Stone nodded and casually left for his consulting room.

Darting her eyes down the list of appointments, she saw one that caught her eye.

"Claire?" Sasha whispered, noticing it was a follow-up booking.

She had crossed so many lines, what was one more? Sasha thought.

Clicking on Claire's medical file was against the rules. Reading it, well that was a whole other matter. Risking everything, Sasha was too inquisitive to not make this final click. So, click she did.

She learned that Claire had seen Dr Stone two weeks ago on a day when Sasha wasn't working. He had then referred her for a scan. A mammogram to be exact. Claire's results were in, and it would only take a couple more clicks for Sasha to learn her friends fate.

"Could you kindly fax this letter off for me please?" asked Dr Stone, reappearing from his office.

"Uh, sure. Yes, of course Doctor" answered Sasha, cleared startled and frantically closing every open window on her computer screen.

'Phew!' she thought to herself, 'that was close.'

To close, Sasha thought, opting to quit snooping and instead, chose to brave a conversation with Claire later that day. Claire wouldn't be expecting to see Sasha at the clinic as it was Sasha's usual day off. Getting on with her duties, Sasha tried to push this new development out of her mind and before she knew it, it was almost 10am, time for Claire to arrive.

Clearly shocked to see Sasha sitting at the reception desk, she stopped suddenly as the door swung closed behind her.

"Hey Claire, you're here for your appointment?"

Claire paused a moment before stepping forward.

"Yeah, I am" she commented back.

"Is Dylan with your Mum?" Sasha asked, making small talk.

"Nah, he is home with James, just chilling out until I get back" answer Claire.

With a nod, Sasha ended the conversation there and Claire chose a seat; seemingly the one furthest away from the reception desk.

With that, Sasha just had to know. She could sense that Claire was nervous, as one would expect and waited patiently before Dr Stone called Claire into his office. Then, in no time at all she had re-opened the file.

Sasha froze, still from head to toe. She couldn't believe what she was reading. Claire was sick. Just how sick, Sasha wasn't sure but from what she was reading, things weren't good.

And then the guilt came crashing back in, almost knocking the air from her lungs. Caught off-guard, Sasha was quickly overwhelmed by the intoxicating shame that came with cheating with your best friend's husband. Her feelings for James didn't contribute to this conclusion. This was all about Claire and how she didn't need this; the burden of her husband's infidelity coupled with this cruel and life-altering disease.

It was a longer journey home than usual as Sasha drove toward the gates of Maggie Creek. She deliberately went slow, trying to concoct reasons why she was leaving, hoping her dad would understand. Sasha felt she couldn't stay, knowing what was likely ahead for Claire, James and baby Dylan. It was bitterly clear to Sasha that she was just a complication, a mistake James didn't need a reminder of every single day. As she neared closer toward the main house, she was sure. There was no way she could stay on after everything that had gone down.

When she reached the main house, it was just past 6pm. Sasha's father was standing outside, leaning against a post. She could see he didn't look good.

Slowing her hatchback down and pulling in front of her family home, Sasha found herself slightly nervous; concerned over the grim look that Frank had written all over his wrinkled face. Suddenly her imagination went into overdrive.

Did he know? She pondered, anxiously. Did he know about Claire? Or even worse, what happened in the hot tin shed last night? Sasha was shaking and so afraid that her father was about to hurl a barrage of disapproval her way. She was sweating, as an amalgamation of various ways to respond to his questioning played on repeat inside her head. With a colossal breath as she climbed out of her car, Sasha approached her father and asked him instantly what was wrong. His response, well it wasn't what she expected at all. It reminded her of the moment she stood frozen in a bathroom cubicle listening to Jess tell her about the passing of their mother. Sasha yet again was being beckoned by that unsettling silence.

"Did you hear me Sash?" questioned Frank. "Sash? Do you hear me?"

Placing her palm on her forehead, Sasha felt her body tremble. A lone tear ran down her right cheek as a river welled in her eyes.

"Yeah Dad", she paused.

"I heard you" Sasha finally said as she turned and peered up at the cottage on the hill.

What she had read about at work was true. Claire was sick, very sick. She had been diagnosed with breast cancer and learning of this felt like triple the blow for Sasha. She had only six months ago, lost her dear mum and Claire had been her closest friend. Sasha grappled with her thoughts for a moment and wondered why this could happen to someone like Claire, someone her own age. They had shared so much together and unbeknown to Claire, they shared a love for the same man.

Sasha instantly felt her world imploding. Her shame turned to a deeper agony. Rapidly, her only concern became how James and Dylan would cope as Frank explained the final details of Claire's diagnosis.

"Claire didn't tell anyone about how she was feelin' darl. There's no way you could have known so don't beat yourself up. Not even James knew. The poor fella" he continued, "the doc says it doesn't look good."

With that news, Sasha fell to her knees and ended up sitting on the front step with her head buried in her hands.

'I am so, so sorry Claire' Sasha thought to herself. An intense pain suffocated her body in its entirety. For a moment there, she could not see a way out of her despair. Once she composed herself, Sasha rose to her feet and held her father tight.

"I'll wait til tomorrow to go and see her dad. Is she going into hospital? What about Dylan?" questioned Sasha.

Frank responded "Yeah, she has more tests to go I think. James mentioned Dylan is going to be staying with Claire's Mum on and off."

That night, Sasha's focus shifted. The hot tin shed, well that was no longer important. The overwhelming fact was, that Claire was Sasha's best friend and there was nothing Sasha wouldn't do to help her friend. The betrayal, albeit serious, no longer warranted her attention.

The next morning, there was a soft knock at the door. Frank was busy in the back garden and Sasha was making breakfast. As she walked around the corner toward the front door she stopped instantly after realising who it was. He would usually just let himself in, thought today was different. Through the fly screen she could see him.

"James…"

He looked poorly as expected and appeared to have had little sleep, if any at all.

"Come…" she ushered, "come inside" Sasha gently prompted.

James opened the door, his eyes were wearier than she had ever seen. His hair was dishevelled and he appeared overwhelming exhausted. James took a small breath in and exhaled. His shoulders were slumped yet he was intently staring into Sasha's eyes.

Within that moment, Sasha yearned to be his shelter, his protector for all his pain; the aching that was quite poignantly cutting him so deep.

"You would have heard?" he whispered as he took a step closer.

Sasha stood there, staring back into his eyes.

"Yeah, I have. I am so very sorry J. I didn't even know she was sick. I had no clue until… Until today" replied Sasha, with tears welling up in her eyes. James took another couple of steps forward and hugged Sasha, squeezing her tight.

"She can't know about us alright? I can't make her suffer any more than she is" he explained.

Sasha understood and the pair decided to push their moment of passion to the backs of their minds. There was no good in telling Claire, it sure would not make her better.

"It's good that Claire's Mum has been able to have Dylan" mentioned Sasha, changing the subject.

"How did you know that?"

"Dad mentioned it"

"Ah I didn't think I'd told anybody that. Maybe he spoke to Claire".

Sasha was sure her father had said that James told him about Dylan but nonetheless, such detail was hardly important.

"Come over and see Claire if you like. I'll have to do some jobs this afternoon" said James, "Why not call by then?"

"You're not taking some time off?"

"Take a look around Sash. This place ain't gonna run itself."

Sasha nodded, and that afternoon she lay on the Lawler's living room floor, stroking Claire's hair as she lay there, vulnerable and fearful for what was to come.

CHAPTER TEN

Don't Let Him Forget Me

Here I sit. Weary and on my own,
thinking about all the hurt that lay
stagnant, waiting for a day that may
never come.

What have I done?

I deserve everything I get.

But, I love him. My first love.

A glorious love that is out of my reach.

Undeservedly here,

Rose

"Sit down here" said Frank, as he poured a cup of tea.

Sasha put down her bag and slumped into a chair.

"You're buggered darl. With work and looking after Claire and Dylan, I think it's time you took care of yourself."

He was right. Sasha had just spent another day behind the desk, and the night before taking care of Claire. This was a regular occurrence as Sasha was spending every spare moment with her friend and baby Dylan.

Getting increasingly unsteady on his feet, Frank

shuffled over to the table, splashing the tea a little as he took each step.

"Here you go, love."

"Thanks Dad."

Sasha cupped her hands around her favourite mug and shifted her knees up toward her chest. It was an unusually chilly evening on Maggie Creek and that cup of tea was definitely what Sasha was craving.

"You read my mind" she said, complimenting her father.

"Are you right to have leftovers tonight? There's still some lasagne from yesterday" said Frank, pointing toward the refrigerator.

Peering up from her cup, Sasha nodded and thanked her father, before he retired to his recliner in the other room. Tonight, she had nowhere else to be. Claire was looked after, and so was little Dylan. So, there she sat; solemn and lost in thought. Following her few minutes of silence, Sasha popped her favourite mug on the sink and walked into the living room. She stood in the doorway for a moment, and took in the sight of her father. His eyes were already closed which wasn't all that unusual for Frank.

As Sasha stared lovingly at her dad, she was sure he didn't know just how much he was loved. Sasha thought back to how he had rejected Jess; how since their mother had gone, everything had changed. Nothing seemed familiar anymore, except the love she had for her father. He may have been hard. He may have not done all he could to be there for Jess. He may have never shown a whole lot of emotion. Yet still, nothing could replace him. He was her dad and that would always count for something.

Sasha pulled her mother's dusky pink throw rug off the couch and lovingly laid it across Frank's lap, before climbing onto the arm of her father's chair and cuddling into him just as she did when she was child. She listened intently to the beat of his heart as his arms reached round and embraced her tight. Sasha was in her safe place, in the arms of the one man who would love her unconditionally. There she remained, for a solid hour before falling asleep in her room, listening to the summer rain, lightly bouncing off the old tin roof.

As the days and months continued to pass, Claire was getting weaker. Her treatment was taking its toll and she kept telling Sasha it wasn't working, and that life was about to change for her family.

"I know I'm nearing my end, Sash" Claire would say, all too regularly for Sasha's liking.

"No, I won't hear that talk! You are a strong. Don't give up" she would always say in response.

Sasha continued to spend most of her time with Claire, helping with Dylan and tending to the day to day care of her friend. That hot summer night would still torment Sasha as she sat long into the evenings by Claire's side. They'd play board games, talk gossip and when Claire was feeling the need, the pair would talk about the future; what it would likely look like with Claire no longer here. Often wrapped in a woollen throw, she was thin, frail and visibly spent. Claire was exhausted from the fight and soon decided that prolonging the inevitable wouldn't do any good.

"Sash, I just need to know my son is going to be okay" explained Claire, laying with her legs stretched out on her sofa.

"I can promise you that Dylan will be just fine. He has a great Dad and an Aunty Sash that loves him to bits."

"Don't let him forget me" said Claire as she gave into her emotions, "He is so little. How will he ever know who I was?"

Sasha moved closer, shook her head and lifted Claire's legs, placing them back down onto her lap.

"I'm not stupid. He won't know me as I was, or as I am. Can you make sure he knows I loved him so, so much? That's all I want. I want him to know I didn't give in easily."

By this time Sasha was fighting back her own myriad of emotions.

"Your son…", she choked.

"He will always know you Claire. You're his mother."

"I also have another request, if that's okay" said Claire, drying the gush of tears that had streamed down her face.

"James deserves to move on. Dylan deserves a

mother. As hard as it is for me to say, when it comes time, make sure James knows that moving on is the right thing to do."

Claire's words burrowed deep into Sasha's conscience.

"That's enough of this talk Claire. You need to stay strong, keeping fighting. Be here for as long as you can be."

Yet still, despite everything, Sasha still was in love with James and behind the scenes, everything was out of control.

CHAPTER ELEVEN

Freshly Picked Apple

Please tell me loving him is not a dream. This insatiable appetite I have to share every little word, every forbidden whisper. His breath on my neck, his pulse next to mine. The words on his lips, as he whisks me even closer toward his shirtless body. Every tender touch takes me in, and little by little I become less of who I was before; more devil, less angel.

I wanted this, but not at the expense of a friend.

Making mistakes, not memories,

Rose

'This isn't okay', she told herself. Yet somehow, some way she continued to ignore those little pigments of decency coming from inside. James was like a freshly picked apple; all shiny yet with imperfections like most other apples on the tree. Yet James' indentations ran deep; a dying wife and a child of not even a year old.

"You know, this can't go on" he'd say to Sasha as she would scramble to button up her open shirt.

His eyes would never look at her during the aftermath of yet another indiscretion. An indecent snippet of time where there wasn't a whole lot of thinking. Just a ravenous, passionate moment; fleeting yet still enough to keep Sasha's attention on him, the man she loved.

They had developed the ultimate affair, if it were such a thing. The pair were stealing moments of passion all over the farm and nobody suspected what was happening, behind closed doors and sometimes in the open air. Frank was busy doing his own thing and Claire, well she was fighting the ultimate fight; the battle to beat her disease.

All this passion somehow meant something during those fleeting moments. Then reality would set in.

Claire.

The mother of his child. His wife. Her best friend. The woman being beaten down by a horrendous illness.

Yet still, after spending time tending to Claire's needs, Sasha and James could not keep their hands off each other. Sasha's guilt was growing, yet not enough to stop.

She knew this was no accidental happiness. Nor was it destiny. This was two people, selfishly connecting for what? For absolutely no good reason at all. Yet Sasha felt that this ride, she was willingly on, was nothing but fate playing catch up with their lives. In her mind, she should have been with James all along.

It was Christmas and both families had come together at Frank's farmhouse. There were all the usual suspects; Frank, Sasha, James, Claire and little Dylan. Also making it to lunch was Claire's Mum, Carolyn.

To everybody's surprise, Jess and her girlfriend, Ally

had flown in from Queensland. To Sasha's delight, Frank had reached out to his eldest daughter, bringing the whole family together for the holidays.

Jess had put on one ripper of a roast lunch with all the trimmings. Sasha had adorned the veranda with cheerful lights and inside the two sisters had put together their old family tree, synthetic and full of school-made ornaments from their childhood. As Jess, Ally and Carolyn prepared the food, Frank was out feeding the chooks. Claire was busy unwrapping gifts with Dylan and well, Sasha and James were recklessly stealing romantic glances when they could.

"Pull me closer" said Sasha as the pair made out behind the door.

She knew that James couldn't resist the scent of her softly tanned skin and the look of her smooth, cherry tainted lips. His kiss would make time stand still, at least in Sasha's mind. The feeling of his breath on her neck would send tingles all throughout her body, each and every time. All she wanted was James and the fact that Claire was sitting in the other room playing with their son meant nothing at all.

"I know you want me" Sasha whispered, as she gently pushed him to the side.

"Let's save this for later" she said in a soft and sensual tone, strolling away and peering back with a cheeky grin.

Walking into the next room, Sasha carried on as if nothing had occurred, even sitting next to Claire on a neighbouring stool. Claire was smiling. These evanescent moments of witnessing Claire playing with Dylan would warm Sasha's heart. It was within these moments that the old Sasha would return, and that guilt would re-appear.

With an intrinsic desire to feel less responsibility than what she knew she should, Sasha pushed her affair with James right down, and only brought it out when she wanted to. The exhilarating pleasure they would create in those moments of betrayal was wrong, deeply wrong and Sasha knew this.

Yet these moments would pass and in her usual fashion, Sasha would tease James, and James would tease back. Then the unthinkable would happen and the cycle would continue. Until the day that everything changed; the moment that their love would be challenged forever.

CHAPTER TWELVE

'come with Me' Eyes

I don't want to think and I needn't make an effort to feel. For what I see in him is the most divine light and I am addicted; hooked to the rush of being in his arms.

So here I remain, cocooned inside this world of love versus deceit; indulgence versus shame.

And I am okay.

As the sun shines brightly on my re-invigorated heart, I can see what he has done for me. I feel free, I feel happy and I am no longer alone.

Waiting for him,

Rose

"Hey Claire! You around?" called Sasha as she reached the white cottage at the top of the hill. It was Saturday and the pair had planned to go out and help repair the old chicken coup next to the cottage. Claire would sit in the sun, watching whilst Sasha hammered away.

After a whirlwind of troubles, Claire had been doing better. She was still not out of the woods, yet not as housebound as she had been for so many months.

Walking on through the back door, Sasha took off her hat. There was Claire, sorting through photos at her kitchen table.

"Hey Claire! It's so hot out there today. Make sure

you bring your hat" Sasha advised, as she took a seat at the table. Claire had been busy printing and placing old photographs in an album. Cancer had made her softer, more in tune with the most important things of all; creating memories and keeping them strong.

"We're doing this for grandma's birthday, hey Dylan?" said Claire, looking down at her baby son who was gnawing on a teething ring, playing happily on the floor.

"Oh, look Sash... Here's a photo of me around Dylan's age. Look how similar we were!" Claire said excitedly, holding a recent photo of Dylan next to an old picture of herself.

Sasha nodded, and gushed over the similarities. The mother and son could have passed as twins! Sasha agreed, thinking Dylan sure did get his enchanting hazel eyes from his mum.

"I can't believe the resemblance! It's spot on!" commented Sasha in delight.

As Claire began to place the photos in a neat pile on the table, Sasha reached down to take baby Dylan in her arms. Feeling his supple, delicate skin, she was in awe of the beautiful family James and his wife had created.

"Oh Claire, he is just so handsome" she whispered, looking lovingly at his sweet little face.

Claire grinned, clearly as proud as punch that she and James had been blessed with such an adorable son. Sasha wanted this, all of it. Oh, how she would have loved this life, she thought. And almost immediately, another gloomy moment of regret came flooding in, taking from this minute of pure joy.

"Mum should get here soon to watch Dylan while we go out to the chook shed" Claire announced.

"It'll be kind of fun to get our hands dirty. I need some time outside."

As Claire's mother arrived, the pair left to complete their chore.

The warmth of the summer humidity was almost unbearable that day. With sweat beats forming all over her body, Sasha pulled away the old chicken wire, exposing the rotting wooden posts. This was a bigger job than Claire and Sasha had first thought. Yet, as the resilient young woman she went about repairing and replacing the damaged pieces. Under Claire's watchful instructions, Sasha put together one impressive home for its residents, who had been waiting in a nearby pen.

Off in the distance, Sasha spotted James flying up toward them on the old beaten four-wheeler. Oh, how he made her weak as he approached, closer and closer. She wiped away the sweat from her brow and shaded her eyes from the piercing sun, watching him ride up toward the coup. As he climbed off the four-wheeler, Sasha couldn't help but stare. His presence made her feel as though Claire had almost disappeared. There he was, just metres away, walking toward Sasha's direction. Almost as if she was the housewife on the hill; just for one split second.

Awaking from her daydream was the moment James

came over and kissed Claire on the cheek. All Sasha could do is stand there in envy, watching the married couple chat about the day.

It was blatantly obvious. He wasn't going to leave Claire for Sasha. She knew that now. Despite her intense jealousy over the loved-up couple, Sasha kept going, working through the next couple of hours, putting the finishing touches on the coup. Call it therapy; call it punishment. She was angry with herself and James, yet that disappointment wouldn't last for long.

After the mammoth task, Claire and Sasha high fived each other in delight. They had turned the rundown chicken coup into a state of the art, rustic masterpiece, complete with a fancy 'Chicks Live Here' sign and an extension, giving the chickens plenty of space to roam.

"I just love it here Sash. I know I don't say it often but we live in the most beautiful place" commented Claire, with one arm wrapped around Sasha's shoulders. They stood there admiring their handy work just for a moment until Sasha headed back down the hill toward the farmhouse. As she stepped inside the front door, Frank was nowhere in sight. He hadn't returned home from town yet so Sasha had the whole house to herself. Until, out of the corner of her eye, she noticed a shadow emerging from the kitchen.

Sasha jumped, not expecting anybody to be in the house. It was James, who had been waiting for Sasha to come home.

"We need to talk" he said, as he ushered Sasha to sit.

"You and I, and this thing we've got. It must stop right now. I have to put my family first and I can't do that if we keep this up."

Sasha looked at James in disbelief. She knew it was over yet wasn't ready to accept their imminent fate. Sasha sat there in silence, unsure of what to say. She looked at him, with her piercing green eyes and said something that she knew he wouldn't have seen coming.

"I am never going to stop loving you J."

James seemed confused, almost dumbfounded by Sasha's calm and almost chilling admission. With that, she got up and headed to the bathroom for a shower. James remained, unsure of how to take Sasha's confession of love.

Looking back at him with 'come with me' eyes, she said those very words. He found it hard to resist, and soon they were in the shower together, their bodies touching as the steam from the hot water fogged the glass. She pushed him up against the wall and kissed him with passion and intent. He liked it, pulling her in as they continued to send each other crazy. They stopped to take a breath, looking at each other, their skin warm and wet. Neither spoke a word, as they reignited the moment and let their selfish instincts take over. Sasha and James made love in the shower that evening, as the sun went down. This was a defining moment in Sasha's mind as she realised something. Her control over James had grown and if she wanted to stop this connection, she could. Though Sasha had no desire to stop. She was convinced it was love, and although James wasn't leaving Claire just yet, she knew he would. She hoped with every part of her being that he would let her go.

CHAPTER THIRTEEN

That Sinking Feeling

This restless road was never one I could have seen me taking. Yet here I am, travelling a distance that should have never begun.

I love him, yes.
But he is not mine to love.
He was never mine to love.

This was the path I chose, and I don't want to walk away.

Still on this ride,

Rose

R unning her bath, after a day in the clinic, she poured a scoop of her favourite lavender scented bath salts into the deep warmth, anticipating how it would soon feel to be enveloped under the water. With a glass of white wine already poured, she was ready to relax. Stripping down to her bare skin, Sasha turned off each tap and took her first step into the old roll top bath. The water was far too hot, yet easing her way in, little by little, took the sting out of the heat.

"I needed this" she whispered to herself, as her eyes innately began to close.

Within seconds, the water had surpassed her shoulders as she melted, ever so slowly down. Sasha exhaled, before taking in the sweet scent of lavender that had begun to envelop the air. She had the lights turned off, with just a single, white candle lit and sitting on the vanity within her view.

Work had been relentless, as Dr Stone's wife was spending more and more time out of the clinic. It was moments like this one where Sasha could just lay there and let go, forget about reality and for a second, return to the old Sasha; before coming back to the farm. Before James.

As she lay there, Sasha began to reminisce. Thoughts flooded her mind about her old life. Her friends, colleagues and the puzzling demise of her relationship with Keir. She wondered where he was, why he'd not ever bothered to give her an explanation. Her life with Keir now seemed like this fantasy that never really happened. Well, a 'fantasy' excluding that dreadful night when everything changed.

Dipping her head under the water and coming back up for air, she wrung out her now long locks with both hands. Steam was rising from the water as she began to emerge up and out of the lavender tainted cocoon that had been keeping her warm. The water was still so hot that she could see the vapours radiating off her naked body, almost like a flame that had just been snuffed out.

There, she would remain until her fingers and toes began to wrinkle, and until her mind began to return into its present day.

Feeling drowsy, Sasha reached for her soft towel as

she stood to get out of the bath. Whilst she patted her body dry and wrapped her hair in the thick towel, Sasha could hear a faint sound coming from her bedroom.

It was her phone.

It was ringing and since it barely rang, she scrambled to cover up and go retrieve it.

The voice on the other end of the phone was Claire. She was crying, and not completely coherent.

"Sasha, I have some news" she said, clearly trying to choke back her tears.

"I'm at the hospital. I'm not so good."

Claire didn't have to say anything else. Sasha knew what that meant.

"No. It can't be" she replied, not wanting to believe the harrowing thoughts that began to enter her head.

"I'll be home tomorrow Sash. They've not given me long."

Sasha dropped the phone and fell back onto her bed.

'This can't be happening' she thought, whilst burying her face into her pillow.

Despite everything with James, Sasha still cared for Claire. In no way did she want her to die.

As the sunlight faded and daylight became darkness, Sasha didn't even notice. Shock shielded her away, instead cocooning her inside a deep, self-inflicted hole. The guilt had returned with vengeance. Finally, Sasha had begun to see that carrying on her affair with James was breaking every single rule. Perhaps too late, she vowed never to go there again.

The next morning, Sasha got up early to the sounds of birds chirping in nearby tress. Waking up after very little shut eye was something she could handle. Though waking up to the new reality that Claire wasn't going to make it, well that was at the very least, intense. Part of her wanted to just escape, run away from the horrible truth. Yet she felt ashamed to be thinking that way. Her rendezvous' with James had certainly not afforded Sasha any rights to be here, during the precious last moments of Claire's life. Yet to preserve whatever Sasha had left, she was forced to stay, as leaving would only bring up a barrage of unanswered questions.

Perhaps staying would be Sasha's punishment or perhaps staying would be the most noble action she could take.

Sitting over on an old bench seat in the garden, Frank had his back to the old farmhouse. Sasha watched him, leaning back, peering up at the clouds as they floated by. He seemed lost, and mesmerised by the blue morning sky.

Sasha wondered for a moment, if with age comes a greater appreciation for these things. For instance, she couldn't recall the last time she had sat in the sun or peered up into the sky, for that matter.

As she approached her father, Sasha noticed something she hadn't seen him do since her mother had passed.

Tears.

Frank was emotional.

Caught in his moment of sadness, he brushed the tears from his weathered cheeks.

"Dad? Are you okay?" asked Sasha, obviously concerned.

Frank didn't speak. Instead, he returned to looking up at the sky.

"Have you heard about Claire?" she continued.

Her father cleared his throat and nodded his head slowly.

Sasha ushered him to shuffle over a little so that the bench seat could hold two. Once sitting, she rested her weary head on Frank's shoulder, and felt the beginning of last night's emotions coming back.

Words didn't have to be spoken. The language expressed within their connection said all that needed to be said.

CHAPTER FOURTEEN

I want to feel the Sun on my face

Oh universe, bring about the strength
she needs to fight this. For Dylan. For
James. For all she is and for all she will
become if given the chance.

Cut into her body, invade it with
whatever will heal my beautiful friend.

So that she may live.

So that she may see her son grow up.

Don't take her from us,
Rose

"Take me outside Sash" said Claire, in a soft, yet broken tone. "I just want to feel the sun on my face."

So, with Dylan on one hip, Sasha wheeled Claire's chair outside onto the front porch. The view was enchanting from outside the cottage on the hill. In the distance, the landscape sung, and the warmth from the sun's gentle glow gave Claire an angel-like radiance. It was almost like the sun shining for Claire that day.

The lush green lawn in the front garden of the cottage was pristine, unlike the rustic feel of Frank's farmhouse garden. Claire's mother, Carolyn was the green thumb. She would spend hours making the gardens that surrounded her daughter's home as lovely, and as colourful as can be. Instinctively Sasha felt the urge to sit Dylan onto the freshly cut grass so he could crawl around free. Claire sat, slightly slumped in her wheelchair in front of her son, watching him pull at the strands of grass.

"Sash, can you please help me down? I want to sit on the grass with Dylan."

Sasha picked up her frail friend's body with care and placed Claire's arms one by one around her neck. She guided her down toward where Dylan was playing, sitting Claire next her son. They played together and as Claire smiled, Dylan grinned back. Sasha sat comfortably next to Dylan, relishing in the pure love between mother and son, all the while trying not to give into the sorrow that framed this otherwise perfect moment.

In the far distance, James was driving up in the white farm ute. Sasha was looking at him, whilst chatting to Claire about how beautiful it was here on the farm.

"Dylan couldn't grow up in a more beautiful place" said Sasha, staring out toward James and the views beyond.

Silence.

The silence drew Sasha to turn and look Claire's way.

Shock, sadness and a desire to change something; anything, came over Sasha. Claire sat slumped over, next to her son. A solitary tear ran down Sasha's cheek.

"Oh Claire" she spoke, with pain radiating from the pit of her stomach.

She reached out to Claire, begging her to wake up.

"Claire!" she said, half whispering her name.

It was too late.

She was gone.

Sasha's attention turned to James again as he came closer and closer.

She placed her arms around Dylan and squeezed him tight, attempting to protect him from the grief.

By this time, James was running toward them.

He knew. He could see the grief in Sasha's expression.

And to make things worse, it was Dylan's first birthday. A day that should have been celebrated yet instead it had become the day that Dylan would lose his mother.

As James reached his wife, he dropped to his knees and held her close, cradling his love within his arms.

James barely made a sound, only a soft whisper in Claire's ear.

"I love you Claire. I love you!" he said.

"No more suffering beautiful, no more."

Sasha held Dylan close, as he squirmed from her grip. Instead crawling over toward his grieving father. James placed his hand onto Dylan's back, whilst still holding his wife firmly against his chest. It was during this moment in time that Sasha realised she had no place here.

She did not belong in this picture. Feeling enormous

guilt and sorrow, Sasha began to back away. Her relationship with James had passed with Claire that day. That insatiable yearning for him had dissipated, leaving Sasha no other option but to go.

CHAPTER FIFTEEN

The Grieving Thief

I held my breath when we said goodbye
As her spirit drifted away,
Oh, how I would have given my all
Just to have her stay.

Nothing I can say will ever bring her
back
Just part of history she will be,
All I have to remember is my regrets
And the kind of friend she was to me.

Oh, how I let you down,

Rose

It had come back around to the Christmas season and Sasha didn't feel particularly festive. In just a week, it was going to be Christmas Day, a time for families to get together, re-group and share their plans for the year ahead. Sasha would be missing out this time, as she had neglected to plan a trip home for the holidays. Instead, she'd find herself doing a whole lot of nothing. Sitting in her petite studio apartment in London, cold and alone.

As Sasha peered through a crack in the curtains late that evening, she caught a glimpse of the happiness below. The streets were packed with people and the atmosphere was pure magic! As she became mesmerised by the glistening lights that were reflecting off the window, Sasha reminded herself of just how alone she

135

truly was that chilly night. There were families out celebrating just being together, yet Sasha had isolated herself from her own.

You see, after Claire died, Sasha could not bear to be stuck out on the farm with only her father and James to talk to. Each time she would venture outside to the front of the main house, Sasha would look left and see the old tin shed and then right, to face the little white cottage perched high up on top of the hill. The shed no longer signified her passionate yet unscrupulous act with James. It had been replaced with the reek of a robust vestige of betrayal; an ache that could never be healed. Each time Sasha would peer up at that little cottage, the only person that she could think about was the friend she lost, Claire.

So, there she now stood, at the foggy high-rise window on the other side of the world, looking down on the hordes people. Sasha knew very well that she was nothing but a selfish runaway; like Keir, the man who left her standing in the rain all those years ago.

On nights when she felt so alone that nothing made sense anymore, Sasha would wait up for an appropriate time to call home. Frank looked forward to calls from his daughter as she neglected to phone often. Sometimes a month would pass and he would hear nothing. Still left in the dark about the true reasons to why Sasha left, Frank believed that his daughter was just off on another adventure. When Sasha left for London, she promised to return however, years had passed and still Sasha had not returned to her childhood home.

Despite making many new friends, landing a great job with the London branch of Cruz Magazine and genuinely paving a life for herself in England, Sasha still felt incomplete. Her longing for James had not left liked she had hoped it would, nor had her immense guilt. Sasha missed her father as well and her constant fear of never seeing him again plagued her more days than she could count. Meeting and finding common ground with new people was easy for Sasha and in an attempt to move on, she did date other men. Though no one was quite like James. He was strong, he was kind, and most of all he made her laugh. That was what Sasha missed most. Sometimes she would find herself daydreaming about going home to Maggie Creek. James would be right there waiting for her, ready to reach out and pull her close. Sasha missed him in every way and each time she'd reminisce about her love, a tingle would run through her body. To Sasha, James was flawless; still her image of the perfect man.

Upon relocating to London, Sasha had born a new existence. She had transformed her appearance all over again, dying her hair a dark almond colour and swapping contact lenses for thick rimmed glasses. The new look suited Sasha and provided her a sophistication that would not have been appreciated back on Maggie Creek. This brand new polished version of Sasha signified a new start yet at the same time, it was a reflection of a woman in hiding. Or at the very least, a woman of reinvention.

CHAPTER SIXTEEN

Dreaming with Eyes wide Open

On the dance floor, I see him standing there. The lights flickering over his face. He's not moving a muscle. He is just there, looking my way.

I take a step forward to gain a better perspective. Yes, it's him. It's the man I left behind.

It's dark inside the club. Yet each time the light shines onto his handsome face I am instantly brought back to when it all began.

I must forget. Leave the past within the past and start living again.

Rose

Sitting stagnant, cold and alone in her bedroom, Sasha reached for her laptop. Seeing familiar faces from all the way back in Australia often made her feel a little closer to home. She'd look forward to these brief moments, chatting with Jess and Ally, who had recently welcomed their own little piece of the happiness puzzle; a baby girl named Eliza. Tiny Eliza was a miracle, born early due to complications with Ally's health. Sasha was heartbroken not to have been there physically during the months that Ally and Eliza spent recovering, although was thankful for the beauty of technology. The fact that Jess could simply video call and send countless photographs was an immense comfort to Sasha who, despite distance, felt more a part of their world than ever before. Playing the role of Aunt Sasha helped her stay connected to the life she left when Claire died. It felt like a small yet special tie to a family she dearly missed.

Waving at the camera, Sasha grinned from ear to ear when her baby niece appeared on the screen.

"Oh, hi beautiful!" she beamed, melting at the sheer sight of darling little Eliza.

"How is she doing?" Sasha asked, looking up for a second to face Jess.

"She is doing so well Sash. Sleeping better which has been a bonus!"

Jess was such a happy new mum, basking in the glory that was parenthood. Ally was coping well and ultimately the couple were just so grateful to have their baby. Ally was still recovering at home as the birth of Eliza was traumatic and took a toll on her body. But she had Jess, and Sasha knew they were so good together.

"Ally is resting at the moment, but things are looking up."

Jess sure had her moments, where things seemed relentlessly disheartening. When she wasn't so sure that she and Ally would get to bring Eliza home. That's where Sasha came in, sending messages of support and encouraging phone calls whenever the new mums needed a friendly ear. There were times when Sasha considered going to Brisbane to help, though in no time, baby Eliza came home and was simply thriving.

Sasha could see that her sister was really embracing

motherhood and everything that came with it. Despite the battles Jess and Ally fought to have Eliza, Sasha knew just how happy they were. And that was all that mattered.

'At least one of us have it all together', Sasha thought, genuinely proud of her big sister.

"Sorry Sash, I'm going to have to cut this short. Somebody has made a mess of herself!" said Jess, signalling it was time to change her daughter.

"Okay" said Sasha, before Jess abruptly ended their call with a smile.

Sasha looked around her room. Suddenly, she found herself all alone again, beginning to wallow in the silence until...

"Ping!"

An email notification popped up on her laptop.

Clicking on the link, Sasha was taken back by the name that was staring her in the face. She gasped, her fingers left the keys and retreated to cover half of her face. Sasha felt that someone has hit the rewind button and suddenly there she was, back in Australia. Back in the city, standing frozen in the midst of a rainy night.

'Keir Sterling' read the name on the screen. Feeling an odd mix of hesitance and curiosity, Sasha clicked to open the email.

'Hello Sasha, I'm sure you never expected to hear from me...'

As she began to read, butterflies were rampant in her stomach. It was nerves.

'Why?' she wondered. Why out of every emotion Sasha could possibly feel was she experiencing this uneasiness? No reason came to mind yet it was so important to her that she read his message in its entirety. Sasha longed to know why he left her that dreadful night though Keir offered no apology and certainly no explanation. A message full of pleasantries was all it was. He wanted to talk and had asked for a reply.

'Do I reply? Do I delete?' Sasha asked herself, grappling with a dilemma she never saw coming.

Deciding to sleep on it, she snapped her laptop shut, rested it on her side table, and turned off her lamp; pulling the covers up until they snuggled around her neck. Sasha barely slept that night, tossing and turning, wondering, imagining... Dreaming with her eyes wide open.

The next morning, awake and utterly exhausted, Sasha poured herself and orange juice and called her supervisor to report that she would not be venturing into work. Today just so happened to be her birthday, yet the last thing she felt like was being sociable. All Sasha wanted to do was sleep and come to terms with last night's blast from the past.

On good terms with her boss, she explained everything, including the reappearance of Keir in her email inbox.

"Vee, I'm not feeling myself today, can you do without me? Combined with the giant bags under my eyes, I'm in desperate need of some cut cucumber and chocolate. Well, the chocolate isn't for my eyes, that's for my hips. I'm sure you get the picture!" rambled Sasha.

"Sasha, relax! It's your birthday and we don't have a lot going on here today. I'll see you at yours, 6pm. I'll bring the chocolates… Oh and the champagne!" replied Vee.

"The champagne?" questioned Sasha.

"Oh, don't question me. I'm the boss! Ciao darling!"

Vee was quick to snap back.

Before Sasha could make another sound, her boss had hung up the phone. It was nothing for Vee to come around equipped with alcohol and good banter, but rarely on a work night. Sasha decided in order to avoid the barrage of questions Vee would likely throw at her, it was easier to just grin and bear it. Keir's email had practically ruined her birthday and Sasha didn't feel like celebrating. Sure, she knew her thoughts on the matter were overly dramatic. But still, now she had this dilemma on her hands. To reply or not to reply. Yet still, in preparation for Vee's grand arrival, she spent half the day cleaning her apartment. Vee, her self-assured, clean and pristine dragon of a friend slash boss, was coming, whether Sasha liked it or not.

CHAPTER SEVENTEEN

Here comes the Queen

I am almost speechless.

Here you are, reaching out to me when you don't even know me anymore.

We are strangers, like those who came to pull me up from the cold, damp cement where you let me fall.

As alone as I am now, nothing compares to the despair of that night.

I craved answers. I begged for them for so long. Yet you never bothered before.

Why now?

I thought you were gone.

Once yours,

Rose

"Darling! I hope you don't mind, but I'm early" said Vee through the intercom in her raspy, posh metropolitan voice.

"It's only just turned 4 o'clock!" replied Sasha, as she reluctantly hit the button to let her up.

"Alright Vee, come in…"

Wearing her designer pant suit, thick makeup and her trademark leopard print wide brimmed hat, Vee strolled through the apartment entrance in a fabulous fashion. She beelined straight to the kitchen.

"Darling! Find me a corkscrew, bubbles await!" she bellowed, whilst fumbling through the drawers in Sasha's petite kitchen.

"Here it is" said Sasha, handing it over to Vee.

She'd already pre-empted Vee's question and dug through the drawers to locate her elusive corkscrew, luckily before her early arrival.

"Sasha, you really do have to do something with these scatter cushions. They are way past due for an update" commented Vee as she threw herself down onto the sofa.

"What's wrong with them?" questioned Sasha, as she peeped over the breakfast bar and admired her chenille 'shag pile style', all suitably in a different shade of beige and white.

Sasha finished up by serving a plate of camembert and crackers then found retreat in her oversize armchair in the corner of the room.

"I know what you're thinking, Vee" said Sasha.

"Now what would that be darling?" Vee responded, pouting her lips.

Scrunching her knees up and pulling her woolly throw rug over and around her arms, Sasha looked noticeably out of sorts. Missing her family over Christmas and now the contact from her old flame had really shook things up for her. Vee understood how it felt to have lost love, having never conquered a relationship longer than a year in all her forty-three years. Despite a lack in flamboyance, Vee saw a lot of herself in Sasha and that's precisely how their work relationship had blossomed into a friendship.

The two spent the next three hours, laughing, crying, clinking glasses and most of all, nattering about their tumultuous loves lives. Sasha didn't know if it was the champagne ruling her head, or her head ruling the champagne but she had decided, with the persuasion lead by Vee, that she would reply to Keir's message. After loading up her laptop, refilling her champagne glass and clunking it down onto the glass top coffee table that sit conveniently in front of her, she began typing letter by letter.

'No fear' she thought, attempting to keep the butterflies at bay.

'Hey there, Keir...' she wrote before pausing and looking directly at Vee.

"No! I can't do it. I just cannot open this up again" Sasha said, shaking her head.

"Sasha! You deserve some kind of retribution for what he did to you! Don't be so weak!" fired back Vee.

"Just engage with him. Don't let him know that you're upset until you sneak up behind him and bite him on the..."

"Stop! Okay, okay. I'll reply. I just don't think I can fake these feelings. I'm still so angry with Keir. He leaving me started a whole host of problems in my life" said Sasha with a weary stare.

Still bothered, yet pushed to take the plunge, she placed her fingers on the keyboard again, and a little like her old journal entries, Sasha felt a freeing feeling; she had finally been given an opportunity to let it all out.

Hi Keir,

You're right. I am very surprised to hear from you. It's been so many years, where has the time gone? To answer your question, I am fine, just fine. I'm living in London, working and right now, desperately missing home. When I say home, I mean the home I retreated to when you left me. After I couldn't find you, I went to live on my family farm.

Do you remember that night?

I do.

Like it was yesterday.

Care to explain?

Sasha

As Sasha stopped typing and hit 'send', Vee swiftly rotated the laptop around.

"Don't look at me like that! I'm your friend, and perhaps your best one at this very moment. I need to see what you said to this clandestine!" said Vee, suitably peeved by what Keir had done to her friend all those years prior.

"He's no clandestine Vee… Bad call. I know he's a lot of things but he wasn't playing around on me" said Sasha, attempting to correct Vee's hyped up version of Keir.

"Okay. He may not be however, he sure was a bloody tosser when he let you go! I would love to give him a piece of my own mind" she angrily responded.

On a few minutes passed by until the laptop went 'ping!' Sasha knew what that meant and quickly jumped up to sit beside Vee on the sofa, tossing her throw rug to the floor as she leapt.

Shocked to see a reply already, the pair begun to skim through Keir's message.

"You are kidding!" said Vee in her boisterous tone. Sasha chimed in. "He expected me to ask so he pre-wrote his message. What's the problem?"

Vee looked as though she was about toss the laptop.

"Oh, Sasha. Sweet, naïve Sasha. It's WHAT he said that is the most frustrating! You don't believe this trollop, do you?" she asked, slightly antagonising Sasha as she continued.

"You were my one and only and I blew it… Or is it the bit where he says he felt like he couldn't breathe? Or perhaps where he tells you he still loves you. Which is it? Sasha, which of his lies are you falling for?"

Desperate for a moment to figure out her own thoughts, Sasha cut Vee off.

"Stop! I don't know. There's still so much that doesn't make sense and I really don't think…"

Vee held her hand up and interrupted Sasha. She had gotten used to her snooty Londoner friend's antagonistic, albeit passionate ways.

"No. Don't give that man another thought. He left you in your darkest moment. How can you possibly give him the time of day?"

Sasha knew that Vee had a point. Yet already, without trepidation, she had fallen for his explanation.

Hook, line and sinker.

Sasha didn't feel romantically connected to Keir anymore but talking to a little piece of her past was intriguing and strangely comforting. It wasn't long until Sasha found herself messaging Keir more and more frequently. She soon developed a great friendship with the man who played a starring role in tearing her world to pieces, only a few short years before.

Every couple of days, Sasha looked forward to a trip down memory lane with Keir. The time difference certainly didn't help and they passed like ships in the night most of the time. They rarely had a few minutes together in cyberspace yet somehow the conversation kept flowing over many months. Sasha learned a lot about

Keir and his new life. He was living in a new city and worked at another leading hospital. Keir spoke a lot about his passion for collecting art and often shared his deep desire to meet with Sasha again.

"I might take a few weeks off work in the Winter here and come over to London. What do you think?" he queried, "I want to see you as I feel like I owe you that much."

Though Sasha never agreed. Her life in London was uncomplicated and drama-free. Sure, she missed her loved ones but as a whole, Sasha had cemented herself in London and was all but a true Brit. The last thing she wanted to do was bring a piece of her past and insert it like a shard of glass into her somewhat easy, new life. Besides, there were still things that didn't add up with Keir. He swore that back when they were together, he was living in that apartment on the 13th floor. Keir's only excuse was that different cleaning staff came through each time and he simply was too busy to introduce himself to every single one.

The part that still remained a mystery was exactly why Keir left that night and when it came time for him to share, he left nothing out.

Rewinding the clock, he started his story right from the beginning; on that balmy Sunday evening at that ultra-trendy garden market in the park. Where he would meet a woman, who caught his eye.

"So, on the way home from work that night, something drew me in. It could have been the prospect of a well-earned drink, the music or who knows? I just needed to disappear into a crowd for a while. It had been one of those days. Whatever it was, meeting you changed my life forever" Keir continued.

"Then I dropped my wallet and what fell out was my most valued item. Not money, nor credit cards, or I.D. That photo you saw? Well that was my wife, Matilda. I had lost her just months earlier, and I wasn't looking for a new partner. Meeting you was..."

He paused, gathering his thoughts.

"It was by chance. I had this beautiful image of Matilda printed small enough to fit in the pocket of my wallet. It was for me. My memories, and suddenly it was flittering away. Until you captured it. You were an angel to me that day."

As he continued to type and send these instant messages, he was touching Sasha's heart. Here was this guy, grieving the loss of his wife and Sasha she never once noticed anything was wrong. At this point, she was again questioning her own self. Reflecting on James, Claire and the way she was so very selfish, Sasha wondered if she had always been this way; so narcissistic that she couldn't see past her own problems. Solemn and apologetic, Sasha blamed herself. She once loved Keir. Then James.

'How could I be so selfish?'

This question kept playing on repeat in her mind. The only two men she had ever fell in love with had experienced such traumatic times and Sasha had never truly known the magnitude of the pain they had faced.

"Can you ever find it in your heart to forgive me?" asked Keir.

"There is nothing to forgive" Sasha assured him, feeling remorse for pain she never knew existed until now. With that, their new online friendship was born and for months, Keir and Sasha kept up with exchanging messages almost daily, reliving their time together and creating new memories.

CHAPTER EIGHTEEN

No Time to wallow

I know I have no right to speak your name, nor suffer because you're gone.

I won't cry for you anymore. I won't say sorry, as I'm sure I could share one thousand apologies and it will never make what I did, right.

For all the storms I may have caused, the one I regret the most is what I did to you and as the strong scent of morning coffee envelops my office, I remember the laughter, the happy times. The days we would sit and natter about anything and everything.

I miss you,

Rose

"Today I feel like an adventure!" said Vee, pulling a lost-looking Sasha out from her chair.

"Stand up! Darling, get your coat. I'm taking you away for the night!"

With a look of 'no way. Do you realise how many wines we drank last night?' written all over her face, Sasha stood defiant.

"That is *not* happening. After work, I'm heading home to a hot shower and a soppy movie" she snapped back, calmly yet direct.

"I won't stand for it! We will stop by your shoebox of an apartment and find you something to wear but that's it! No more of this. I've booked everything!"

Like that, Sasha's spontaneity sparked and she leaped out of her seat.

"Well, I guess if the boss says so, I'm in!" she exclaimed, with a glimmer of nervous excitement.

"We will be spending one glorious night in this cute, chic hotel I found online, followed by the most magical day of your life!" said Vee, as she swished her kaftan in Sasha's face. "I'm taking you to my happy place, a place that everybody who finds themselves in a rut must go."

"Oh, you mean to Kings Road, or is it one of your other favourite shopping strips?" quipped Sasha, half joking, though she would hardly be surprised if this was the actual truth.

"No!" Vee said, in her discerning accent, "We are not going shopping. You just wait and see! This may surprise you but I was like you once. Wallowing over some man."

Sasha looked at Vee, puzzled, and quite clearly in denial.

"But I'm not."

"Oh, but you are, and I am taking it upon myself to change that. Now follow me!" quipped Vee, not standing for Sasha's defiance.

Walking out of Cruz Magazine when it has just past 9am was liberating. Sasha strutted with an air about her that squealed 'freedom' in capital letters. Vee had a car waiting just a few doors up, a Rolls Royce of course and as Sasha was led toward the car, she peered down at her phone.

"Turn that off! This is for your own good!" Vee snapped, attempting to snatch it from Sasha's grasp.

In what felt like no time at all, Sasha and Vee found themselves in the Wiltshire countryside, drinking up the charming scenery, laughing, telling stories and having the best day.

Vee promised that tomorrow would change Sasha's life and that was quite the promise. Sasha didn't really know what to expect from Vee as quite frankly, she had never seen her friend in the country and would never have pictured such a scene. Vee was the kind of woman who like the finer things in life, a city dweller through and through. She had chosen career over raising her only daughter, total freedom over marriage and status over everything. Shallow perhaps, but nonetheless a great mentor to Sasha. A woman who hadn't quit punishing herself for past mistakes; a woman who was yet to find her truth.

The next morning after waking from the dreamiest sleep, Sasha stretched her arms above her head.

"No alarm" she whispered, without a clue to what the time may be.

From the next room she could smell food, and knew instantly that a freshly cooked breakfast was waiting there, ready to be devoured. Sitting up and slipping her on her silk kimono style gown (a Christmas gift from Vee) and tying it at the front, Sasha ran her fingers through her hair and made her way out to the living room. There sat Vee, in front of an array of fresh fruits and warm plates of delicious food; too much for any two people to eat. Sasha peered up from all she could describe as 'food art' and smiled at her friend.

"Really Vee? This looks divine, but excessive!"

She sat down, and began to fill her empty plate with breakfast.

"What time is?" Sasha asked, inquisitively.

Vee grinned.

"Oh, I thought you would ask that. Now brace yourself. It's 5am."

Sasha dropped her cutlery and it clunked suddenly onto her plate.

"What?! It feels later than that. Wow. Okay. This no phones rule has totally thrown me!"

Vee continued to smile at Sasha and instructed her to eat up or the pair would be late.

"Where are we going?" asked Sasha, who was bursting with questions.

"Eat!" exclaimed Vee, not ready to let go of the surprise.

And in what felt like no time at all, Sasha and Vee were looking their Winter best and ready to go.

CHAPTER NINETEEN

Magic in the winter

I am lost in a forest of my own thoughts.
Tangled in a web of weeds. I have
nobody to blame, for this endless shame.
For I weaved these weeds myself.

Searching for a way out,

Rose

She stood there, before one of the most beautiful sights she had ever seen; possibly the most stunning in the world. She stood there wondering how a woman so flawed could be as blessed as she was at that moment, standing there with an open heart and soaking in so much precious energy. It was at that very moment Sasha began feeling her mother's presence; so warm and oh so strong. It was as though her mum had wrapped her loving arms around Sasha's shoulders, calming her, forgiving her daughter; finally allowing her to feel at ease. It was bitterly cold, yet as the sun began to rise in the distance, the warmth she could feel enveloped her and Sasha knew, for if this was not the loving embrace of her mother, it was most certainly a pleasant thought.

She imagined her mum standing there by the mysterious stones. Seeing her strong and nurturing mother created a rush of emotions – all comforting; and Sasha took that time to feel the immersion of love that her mother had for her. She couldn't help but wonder if after all she had been through – and put others through, that she was led to this very spot in the midst of the Wiltshire countryside. All the guilt, shame, sadness and trepidation from the past begun to melt away, setting Sasha free.

Her spiritual connection to her mother became stronger with every breath. The warmth of her beloved mum, and even the scent of her perfume took Sasha back to the days when her mum was just a bus ride away. In what felt like no time at all, Sasha knew; she just knew that her mother was right there with her that chilly morning. Her senses grew stronger, and reassured Sasha as she delved deep into her own hiatus. In her view were the glorious stones of Stonehenge and on her mind, was her much loved, and much missed mother. Sasha knew, with all her heart, that Maggie was right there by her side; healing Sasha of all her self-inflicted torment.

'I don't want to punish myself anymore' she thought as the Winter sun began to gleam across the icy hillside.

Although she could not actually see her mother, nor articulate quite how special this moment was, it was real. It was real to Sasha.

With a fire in her belly, Sasha was ready. Ready to

take on the world. It was time to forgive herself and to pave her own path, without holding onto past mistakes.

As Sasha turned to thank Vee, she was welcomed with a hug.

"So darling, it worked then?" Vee questioned, assessing the effective of her magic night away.

"Yes Vee. And this is only just the start."

CHAPTER TWENTY

Fire in her Belly

A new year has begun and with that, has come this new me. A better version, a more well-rounded me.

Swerving to duck from the double-edged sword of guilt that keeps me on my toes, I shudder to think what life would be like if I had remained in Australia. I have dodged my responsibilities for long enough. It's time, like my mother would say, to move past all of this.

Whatever it takes, I am going to get through it.

Finally remorseful,

Rose

T hat familiar hot coffee aroma occupied the air, as Sasha went about her morning office rituals. Armed with a cup of strong black tea, a slice of raisin toast and some mints for later, she was ready to trudge through her day. A quaint, little deli conveniently located between Cruz Magazine and the tube station had become her go-to spot for all she needed to keep her day productive, and as a creature of habit, Sasha thrived off the repetitiveness.

There were never many people in the office when Sasha would arrive, greeting Pierre the cleaner as they passed each other by the elevators. Sasha would ask him how that gorgeous grandbaby of his was, and they'd talk briefly about the state of the economy, the weather or some other mundane topic. Being early came with its advantages, as Sasha enjoyed that first half an hour, preparing for the whirlwind that would soon come swaggering through the double glass doors.

As Vee's executive assistant, Sasha's role was to oversee just about everything that went on at Cruz, from the receipt of office supplies to major deal negotiations. She certainly wasn't short of things to do. Vee's personal list of tasks alone kept Sasha occupied.

- *Drop off dry cleaning*

- *Pay 'Chanel the Chihuahua's' doggie day-care bill*

- *Send birthday gifts to Isabel*

The list often seemed endless yet one of Sasha's favourite tasks was visiting expensive stores to find ideals gifts for Vee's 15-year-old daughter, who was away living an affluent life in East Horsley with her father. Vee barely spoke about Isabel and rarely gave an insight into why she wasn't living in Surrey herself. Nevertheless, if Vee wanted something done, Sasha would deliver. No questions asked.

Being good friends with the boss also had its perks. The parties, the sample beauty products, the booze... It all became a welcome distraction for Sasha as she continued to pave a life for herself in London. Every day was the same, yet that's how generally liked it.

Today was just like any other. After consulting her

schedule, Sasha began working on task number one. Placing her fingers on the keyboard, she begun following up on emails. For some unknown reason, the sound of the keys clicking away seemed louder today.

Tap, tap, tap, tap, tap, tap, tap, tap, tap.

The succession of sounds played like a marching band on fast forward, until the words she was typing became jumbled and unrecognisable. Sasha couldn't help herself. She kept reflecting to Stonehenge and how the abundance of energy and light gifted to her seemed to be depleting. It had gotten her through a lonely holiday season, and now there she sat. Flat.

Totally and utterly drained.

Almost back to where she started.

Confusion over why she was feeling so empty, when she had so very much, was playing on repeat in her mind. Sasha felt like a fool, sitting there, with the flourishing career, great friends and that brand-new life she'd hoped would be her way out.

Stopping to take a long, slow sip of her tea, Sasha closed her eyes for a second.

'What am I missing?' she pondered, with the answer to her question almost right on the tip of her tongue.

She had the job. Tick. The friends. Tick. Sure, no serious relationship yet but in her heart Sasha knew that would come. Besides, this yearning was for something else; something she couldn't quite put her finger on.

All the sudden, Sasha jumped at the sound of Vee's

voice, waking her up from a brief moment of reflection.

"Darling, fetch me some coffee, would you?" she said, tossing her plaid wool coat across her assistant's desk, almost spilling Sasha's tea.

"Watch it!" she shrieked, carefully moving her cup.

Vee covered her mouth with the tips of her fingers.

"Oh, sorry darling!" apologised Vee, raising her perfect eyebrows ever so slightly.

"There is simply no time to waste. Forget the coffee! I need you in here to take notes, stat!"

As Vee strutted into her glass box of an office, Sasha sighed, before following her in.

She watched on whilst Vee sat down in her comfy leather chair, slipped off her designer red heels and knelt her bony elbows onto her glass desk.

"Please sit" instructed Vee, pointing to the chair that sat adjacent.

As Vee began to narrate, Sasha began to escape again. She was on her own cloud, trying very hard to picture whatever it was she was missing.

"… And I want to make abundantly sure that we do not run anymore of Freya's rubbish story ideas. She truly has developed a penchant for disappointing me and I just cannot bring myself to..." a quick speaking Vee stopped, mid-sentence.

"Sasha, are you with me?" she asked, with a puzzled expression.

Sasha immediately sat further upright in the chair.

"Yes, yes. Sorry, Vee. I've got it. We're cutting Freya from this month's edition" answered Sasha, feeling emotionally dishevelled and hoping there was nothing else Vee had mentioned.

"What's wrong?" Vee asked, cutting to the chase.

"Nothing" said Sasha, plonking the world's worst attempt at a fake smile onto her face.

"Let me see" said Vee, leaning in, almost analysing Sasha's expression.

"You're not happy. I think I know what will help. Allow me to tell you a story."

With that, Sasha pulled her chair in closer, resting her notepad and pen on Vee's desk.

"When I was younger, I didn't know what I wanted. I had no ambition and I was nothing like you. Yet, I was also everything like you. I was brought up to believe that my job on this earth was to meet a nice man, get married and raise a family. Does that even sound like me? Answer, truthfully."

Sasha cautiously answered.

"No."

"That's because when I had accomplished these things, I realised something. I was never meant to be a wife, nor a mother. I was put on this earth for other reasons and at that time was just too young to realise that when I was blundering my way through life, that very thing, my life, was passing me by."

Sasha gently nodded, and felt intrigued to hear more of Vee's story.

"And I was judged. Judged harshly for this. My family turned their back on me and Sebastian, well he was less than thrilled about my decision."

"Who is Sebastian?" asked Sasha.

"The father of my daughter." Vee answered, without delay.

"As painful as it was, and as gut wrenching as it still is for me to admit, Isabel was better off in a family who loved her, regardless of how that family would go onto be formed. I had to be fearless. I had to make a decision and stick with it."

Vee continued.

"There was simply no turning back."
Sasha looked shell-shocked. She had never had the privilege of hearing this story before.

"Oh Vee. I didn't know. I had no idea why you didn't have Isabel living with you and always felt it wasn't really my place to ask."

Vee pursed her lips, before letting out a gentle smile, and continuing her story.

"I've travelled the world, Sasha. I've been to every corner. All the while, Isabel has been raised by a father who loves her, and a mother who adores her. She has two parents. I am just not one of them."

"So, your ex-husband remarried?" probed Sasha.

"We never married. He met Christina a year after I left. Since then, Isabel has known Christina has her mother, and me, well, I'm just Vee."

Clearing her throat, Vee went on. Despite being far from similar to Sasha's own journey, Vee's words somehow echoed her situation. Vee had Sasha enthralled, yet sad. Heartbroken for Isabel, Sebastian and Vee; a family that could never be.

"So, now to my point. I abandoned my own flesh and blood because I was selfish, but I'm okay with that now. Sometimes, as brutal as it sounds, we must be selfish. It took time, but within that time came peace. If I hadn't left, Isabel wouldn't have had all she has now."

"Does she know you're her birth mother?" asked Sasha.

"Yes, she does. Isabel has always known. There will come a time when I will probably have to face what I did and it may not be pretty. But with these kinds of choices, come consequences. You need to know that what you're running from does not have to frame your entire existence. Forgive yourself, and move on at once!"

Vee continued, expressing her stern advice with fierce.

"If there is a God, let him judge you. Stop trying to perform that role for yourself."

Her words continued to resonate with Sasha. She had been so busy trying to escape, rather than face what she had done.

179

"Vee, you have never spoken such truer words. I need to take some time to figure out my next move. I can't keep this up much longer."

"I will give you that time. Now dear Sasha, I want you to go. Find whatever you're looking for and return when you've found it."

'Said no boss ever' thought Sasha, looking Vee in the eye, seeing whether she was serious.

"I mean it. One week, two weeks, a month. I don't mind. I care about you too much just to watch you sit here, amongst the drudgery of your own sad existence. You've built yourself this prison. Now it's time to use the key and leave. Or better still, tear the whole wretched thing down!"

There it was again. That rush of energy Sasha inherited from her time standing by Stonehenge.

"Who will do my job?! Vee, you need me. I can't just go like this."

Vee raised her hand, shunning from Sasha's excuses.

"Freya cannot write a good story to save herself. Maybe she can run my errands. Honestly, how could I ever replace you darling? Cruz Magazine will be fine. It's fine. Go, fly free. Be spontaneous! Live your life!"

Sasha in what felt like no time at all, was standing on the street outside the building, unsure of what was next; yet excited about what was to come.

CHAPTER TWENTY-ONE

Fly Free

Standing with my heels dug into this concrete palace, I stare. Watching the passers-by, their eyes firmly on their destinations.

I take a breath in this murky, but pretty city.

It's time for me to fly free.

Watch me bloom,

Rose

As she peered over the book display, there he was. Hot Spanish guy from the office. She had never uttered a word to him before, just admired the fine-looking gentleman from afar. He formed part of the Arts Department, and since Cruz Magazine was a large conglomerate, Sasha didn't really have a reason to speak with him. All her communications with this department was done through hot Spanish guy's not-so-hot boss, Stan who was lead designer at the magazine.

Sasha had just been instructed to 'fly free' and perhaps this was her opportunity to do just that. Feeling courageous, she walked casually around the display in an effort to bump into him. And her tactic worked! Immediately hot Spanish guy looked her way. His smile was infectious and those eyes, well they seemed to have the power to draw Sasha in, as close as socially acceptable.

"Are you into world politics?" he asked, in his hot Spanish guy accent.

Without realising, Sasha had picked the worst conversation piece to stand in front of. She had gone into the store to find a good book to pass the time, instead Sasha had become too distracted by the idea of clinching a good-looking man. She fumbled, placing the book she had innately picked up, back down onto the shelf.

"Ha, well not really. I'm more into…" she paused, peering over to catch a glimpse at what kind of book hot Spanish guy had in his hand.

"Ah... Young adult fiction?"

Her answer turned into a bizarre open-ended question.

Catching on, hot Spanish guy quickly explained.

"This is for my niece, Manuela. It's her birthday this Saturday."

Sasha chuckled, and admitted she certainly wasn't into young adult fiction. Placing Manuela's birthday gift under his arm, hot Spanish guy stopped to introduce himself.

"Anyway, it's a pleasure to meet you", she said, holding out his right hand.

"My name is Rafael. I've notice you in our office."

Sasha leaned in to shake Rafael's hand, his grip

pulled her in that tiny bit closer.

"My name is Sasha. I'm sorry, this is embarrassing. My friend told me it would feel good to be spontaneous but clearly I'm not doing this right!"

Sasha stumbled across her words, trying to explain away her awkwardness; butterflies tangled in her stomach.

His smile grew wider, and the pair struck up a conversation. They talked about their favourite books and about work, until their conversation led them to sipping tea and sharing red velvet cake at the bookshop café located in the centre of the store. He was a writer and she was a writer. Sasha rarely shared that with anybody. He had been working on a novel, she too had been working on her very own piece of writing.

"I don't really have the end product in mind but I do write down my thoughts regularly" she said, hinting at her long-standing journal.

"Ah, so you're not writing a book, yet you are writing a book. That makes sense" laughed Rafael, in a jovial tone.

Sasha looked back bashfully, not wanting to give it all away. Yet he was quite right about something. Sasha hadn't thought about how she could shape her journal entries into her very own book.

'What a neat idea' she thought to herself.

"I have a whole heap of material. Perhaps someday I might turn it into something."

Rafael, with his permanent hot Spanish smile

plastered on his face, reached out to hold Sasha's hand. In an instant, Sasha noticed that his hands were soft and his grip was strong. She felt herself move an inch closer to hear Rafael's words.

"So, what is stopping you? I mean, you are here. You have the words. Why not share them?"

And with that, Sasha's stomach was swarming with those pesky butterflies again. Here was this stranger across from her, giving her the next jewel of wisdom that Sasha needed in her plight to move on.

"I'm going to my sister's holiday villa in the Canary Islands this evening. We are meeting there for Manuela's birthday" Rafael explained.

"Come with me."

Sasha's eyes widened.

"What?"

Rafael looked at her with intent. She could tell he meant what he was saying.

"All your talk of spontaneity has got me feeling spontaneous!" he announced, almost bouncing out of his seat.

"I've known you..."

Sasha starred over at an old wooden clock on the far wall and repeated herself.

"I've known you for no more than two hours and you're asking me to come away with you?!"

Undeterred Rafael persisted.

"Well, why not? I like you. You like me. I write. You write. Let's write together!"

Sasha couldn't help but grin. He had her excited and as he spoke, she tried not to let him see it.

"What about your family?" she asked.

"I'm going a week earlier so I can work on my book. I would love for you to come. One week in the sun. How could you resist?"

Sasha was completely enamoured by his spell. Filled with adrenalin and feeling impulsive, she agreed and in a short time she had been back to her apartment, packed her suitcase and was on her way to meet Rafael at the airport. Sure, throughout the process of packing to go away with a stranger, doubts and trepidation flooded her head. Though not enough to overrun the intense feelings telling her to just go for it.

As they entered check-in, the pair resembled a loved-up couple about to embark on their honeymoon. Little did anyone around them know that Sasha and Rafael had only spoken for the first time just a few short hours before. This was part of the excitement, thought Sasha as she laughed at his jokes, brushing his arm and staying close. She could tell by the way he looked at her, that Rafael was feeling it too; a connection. An impulse to be as close to Sasha as he could get. Sasha felt invincible, and a mere shadow of the woman who sat idle at her desk that very morning.

CHAPTER TWENTY-TWO

La Gomera

He slid his index finger slowly from the top of her forehead, all the way down her nose, over the ripples of her mouth, down past her chin and neck; until he stopped at her chest. His glare, fuelled by immense passion, met with hers. She imagined being whisked into his strong, tanned arms, kissing him with her soft, crimson lips.

Yes, I know. A little cliché but this is how I'm feeling!

Amor,

Rose

Arriving at Rafael's family villa that next morning, was magical. The sun was shining and the air was warm. The villa's crisp white exterior was modern and gave little away. As Rafael's hire car pulled into the vast, underground garage, nothing could have prepared Sasha for what would come next.

As they reached the ground level, Sasha was utterly in awe of the sight before her.

"When you said villa, this is not what I imagined!" she said with delight written all over her face.

The glorious view beyond and liquid white floors drew Sasha in. As she walked toward the expansive ocean scenery and slid open the floor to ceiling glass doors. The girl from country New South Wales was met with even more surprises; a private plunge pool and garden that most would only dream about. Turning back to face Rafael, Sasha shone with happiness. Perusing the room with her eyes, she could see this was no ordinary holiday home. This was something else.

"Raf" she called, distinctively branding her new friend a nickname.

"You have got to be kidding. This place is beautiful!"

"You haven't seen it all yet" Rafael replied, with that trademark grin shining back in her direction.

He then took Sasha's hand and led her from room to room.

"There are three bedrooms, two on this floor and another above. We're just a short drive to the village of Playa de Santiago where I'd love to take you out for dinner while we are here."

Blushing, Sasha accepted and the pair planned to go out that evening. In the meantime, Sasha explored the villa and admired the views. She was unsure as to how she got here, yet simply captivated and living in the moment.

Walking out onto the gloriously green garden, Sasha admired the colourful array of blooms. She was a long way from home and was determined to try and forget about her worries, and delve deep into the La Gomera sunshine. Soon, Rafael appeared, wearing nothing but swimming shorts. Plunging his body into the pool and shaking back his dark hair, he invited Sasha in. She didn't need much convincing and quickly went inside to change.

'A mid-morning swim is just what I need' she felt, walking into one the three very luxurious, sunlit bedrooms. Double doors met the outside space where Rafael relaxed in the pool. With every splash and movement he made, Sasha got excited. He was handsome and she could have never imagined how her daring, yet clumsy attempt to chat him up would land her right here in this moment.

Soon she found herself in the pool with Rafael, enjoying champagne in the morning and watching the water beyond. He was charming and not just that, he was interesting. Sasha was intrigued by this man. He spoke of his love for writing and finding inspiration wherever he went.

"Today, you will be my inspiration" Rafael announced, holding Sasha close. She was utterly floored by his presence, let alone his words. His breath on her body, the warm sun on her back. Rafael had Sasha's full attention.

After drying off and showering, one after the other, Sasha sat down at the dining table with just a pen and loose paper. Rafael sat opposite her.

"Now just free write whatever comes to your mind" he instructed, as Sasha nervously agreed.

As Rafael put his head down, he began to scribble his words onto the page. Sasha, on the other hand, stared blankly without a clue on what to write. Rafael was busy in his writer's trance and too enthralled for a moment to notice she was struggling. Though when he did, he offered more words of wisdom.

"Let go. If your sentences don't come out so well, that's good. This is a process. In time, they'll all make perfect sense."

So, with that, she began by picking up her pen again and putting it to the page.

Then nothing. She was blank.

Rafael took her right hand and removed the pen from her grasp.

"Stop" he gently said, clicking his fingers in front of his face and demanding her focus. Sasha's eyes shifted from the page to Rafael's stare.

"You need to learn to be present in this moment. This moment only. Forget who you should be. Who you were. Where you've been. What you've done and just be, be you. Be real. Be your pure self."

His deep words tugged at her heart. Rafael was right. Sasha knew that she had to learn to let go and that through her writing this was possible. As he released her trembling hand, she immediately picked up her pen again, with all eyes still on the man before her.

"Remember, moments like these are evanescent. They are fleeting, they a brief. Take advantage of it" he said, before letting go of her hand.

'Those eyes' she thought to herself before speaking.

"I know exactly what I want to express. Their connection went on despite both Sasha and Rafael breaking their mutual stare. The new friends began to pour all their energy onto their respective sheets of paper. What began as a one-page exercise, grew. With her hand throbbing, Sasha continued, taking a second piece of paper, and then a third. She had no idea if her words were making sense but this was therapeutic.

Sasha and Rafael didn't make it out for dinner that night. Instead, they continued to pour out their creativity, until retiring to the pair of chaise lounges that sat by the illuminated pool.

"That was amazing, Raf" whispered Sasha, as she lay there, feeling serene, watching the reflections coming off the water.

"If this is day one, I can't even imagine how I'll feel by the end of this week" she continued, sitting upright to face her friend.

Rafael rolled onto his side to get a good look at Sasha, and laid the palm of his hand gently down onto her bare thigh. Tingles made their way through her body like electricity. He had this power over her that simply brought Sasha to her knees.

Sitting up and looking Sasha directly in the eye, Rafael encouraged her to lay back down on the chair. He slowly guided her body down, back to how she was laying before. Placing his hand on her stomach, Rafael made Sasha feel calm. Almost instantly, she became aware of every breath, watching his hand rise up and down. Over and over again.

"Close your eyes" he quietly instructed, and for some

reason Sasha felt compelled to do everything Rafael said.

"Listen to my voice."

With his right palm lying motionless on her stomach, he began to stroke her forehead with his fingers.

"Listen to the water. You are so close, you can almost touch it with the tips of your toes."

Suddenly Rafael's hands drifted away and there Sasha remained, feeling every breath, escaping subconsciously to the water's edge.

"Listen deep to the intrinsic sounds that try to evade your ears. The waves, the soft, warm breeze. Even the soft crackling of the sand cradling your entire body."

At this point, Sasha was completely immersed in the moment. She could see herself on that beach; naked, alone and purely at ease.

"Take a minute. See for yourself. That sun piercing down, warming your heart with its rays. Ask the sun to bring you all the energy you need to be creative, to live a full life."

Sasha continued to listen intently as Rafael took her to a meditative place she had never been before. After waking from her reverie, Sasha felt that energy surge again. Just like those feelings she evoked at Stonehenge.

As the days went on, Sasha joined in on Rafael's daily meditation rituals. They shared their dreams, wrote stories for hours, took long walks and made insatiable love every single night. As Rafael said, these moments were to be fleeting, so Sasha took them and made the most of every one.

He made her laugh unlike any other man before him. A graphic designer, a writer and an avid dreamer, Rafael told Sasha of every dream he ever had and every single one he'd already conquered.

Rafael learned at a very young age that the word 'hope' wasn't at all what it was cracked up to be.

"Why sit around and hope for things to change when we all have the power to do something" he said.

Sasha didn't agree.

"No disrespect meant but how can you say that? You're sitting in your very expensive villa in the Canary Islands. Hope is often all that a person has."

"This is not my villa. This belongs to my sister and her husband. She and he made something out of nothing. Not once did they sit around and hope."

His response stung a little.

"Look, all I'm saying Raf is that some people really cling onto hope."

Rafael shook his head.

"Yes, they do, but if they don't do anything to change things, hope will mean nothing in the end."

Whether they agreed with each other or not, this made no difference to Sasha who couldn't help but be attracted to Rafael's proactive attitude towards life. She reflected on this when later that night, whilst running her fingers over his shoulders, as he poured her a cup of herbal tea. Making her way down his chest and towards his hips, she cupped his body close.

As Sasha peeled off his white linen shirt to reveal his toned back, she squeezed Rafael closer, to feel the warmth radiating from his body. She hadn't noticed before now the small tattoo on his right shoulder; a fire breathing dragon with a spear in its hand.

'Was it symbolic?' she pondered, and without a second thought began to place her manicured fingernails onto Rafael's biceps, walking them all the way back up to his shoulders.

Pulling him in even closer, she could hear every breath coming from Rafael. They were becoming longer and faster. Sasha gently kissed the right side of his neck, before spinning him around. Moments later, the pair were in the bedroom where Rafael melted onto the bed like ice. The scent of his bare skin reminded Sasha of James for a second, yet soon she lost every inhibition. Her thoughts of James turned to mush and it became all about Sasha and Rafael; his words 'moments like these are evanescent' sung on replay inside her head.

As Rafael began to slide down the straps of Sasha's sun dress, she shivered in delight. His mouth kissing her so tenderly as he grasped onto her hips. They took it slow, giving life to the electricity that intensified with each and every touch. She kissed him back, on his chest and all the way up to his ear. With every kiss he would plant on her body, Sasha melted even more.

Pushing her gently down onto the bed and urging her to turn onto her stomach, Rafael began to relax her, taking Sasha to a place of, pure, unadulterated bliss. His hands did all the talking, as he made his way from her neck, right down to her toes. His massaging hands led Sasha to feel totally at peace.

After they made love, Sasha sipped a new cup of tea and chatted with Rafael. Their conversation surpassed her cup of tea and went on for hours.

Sasha was just so blissfully happy. To be with Rafael, no matter how fleeting her moment in the sun with him would be.

CHAPTER TWENTY-THREE

I Didn't Even Know

I feel as though I've been drifting about on a cloud since flying home to London. As I touched down in my favourite city in the world, I look back with gratitude. Rafael breathed fresh air into my lungs and brought me back to life. I can now live without the guilt and put my energy into better things — My writing, for one!

Still not quite ready to resurface,

Rose

Arriving home from the airport, Sasha got out of the cab, pulling her small suitcase over the crevices in the concrete. Clearly, she had caught Rafael's infectious smile as she was beaming from ear to ear. Meeting Rafael had changed everything for Sasha and finally, she was beginning to see what she wanted from this life. As Sasha made her way up to her third-floor apartment, she opened the door. A pungent smell of rotting food brought her back to reality as it wafted from the kitchen. Sasha was swift to realise that she had left food out on the counter.

"Yuck!" she said, dropping her suitcase and quickly scurrying to find something to clean up the mess.

Desperate to check her messages, Sasha detoured to place her phone on charge. She had just spent the entire week without a working phone as she had neglected to pack her charger. Not exactly the most sensible thing to do given the fact she had just travelled abroad with a stranger.

While drowning her kitchen bench with disinfectant spray, Sasha was on standby to hear a multitude of notifications 'dinging' away as her phone began to turn on. After tapping a few buttons, soon she was listening to her voice messages, one after another. And there were multiple messages from her sister, Jess.

"Hi Sash, it's Jess. Look, there's no easy way to say this but there's something you need to know about Dad. I'm down at the farm at the moment as I got a call from Dad last week. I took him into Dr. Stones' office today and we've just received results back. Dad's got Alzheimer's Disease. I'm sorry Sasha, I would have liked to tell you in person but this will have to do. Maybe if you can afford the time off work, you could come and see Dad? Anyway, let me know. You know my number. Where are you by the way? I'm beginning to get worried."

Sasha's jaw had hit the floor. Her worst nightmare.

'Not my Dad!' Sasha thought as she scrambled to find Jess' phone number in her contacts list.

"This can't be happening!" she said out loud.

Unable to get in touch with her sister, Sasha rushed over to her laptop and searched frantically for an affordable flight home. On such short notice, this would prove to be a tough task. Finding a flight would be the easy part. Making sure it fit within her meagre budget would not be so breezy.

Sasha ran back over to her phone, and tried to call her father.

"No answer" she said to herself.

"I didn't even know he was sick."

Sasha was panicking.

'How did I not know? What sort of daughter am I?'

Her mind was going crazy. She hadn't called him in a while. Guilt crept back in, and made Sasha even more determined to get back home to the farm.

"Bingo!" she said, locating a seat on the quickest flight she could find, departing the next day.

Sasha tried to call her sister again. And again, leaving a message this time.

"I'm coming home sis. See you in a few days."

Her message was short and sweet.

Amongst all this self-amplified chaos, Sasha had been in touch with Vee and of course she was understanding. Vee also was curious as to where Sasha had been all week. Sasha gave little away, just that she had been to Spain.

"I have to see you darling! Meet me at the piano bar at 8."

Sasha went to respond with a polite 'no thanks' but Vee wouldn't hear of it. So as day became night, Sasha made her way to their favourite bar on Kensington High Street. The pair nattered away for hours, and Sasha left no detail out.

"I never knew it was possible to be that happy" beamed Sasha, after relaying her week-long rendezvous with Rafael.

"I now realise how desperately I needed to shake things up."

After her night out with Vee came to a close, Sasha took a taxi home. Tucking herself under her warm, thick quilt, she closed her eyes. All Sasha could think about was her dad and how she hadn't been there in the way she should have been.

"Stop" she whispered, placing her palm on her stomach before transporting herself back to that La Gomera beach. She pictured the dominating, blue sky above, and enjoyed the feeling of the water tickling her feet; the warm sand supporting her body from head to toe.

Waking that next morning, Sasha felt refreshed, despite the red wine from the night before. She had a text from Jess who was very excited about Sasha's impending trip home. Then finally, when it was time get on that plane, Sasha was more than ready. She was just so keen to get home to see her dad.

CHAPTER TWENTY-FOUR

Coming Home

Like a free and whimsical butterfly
I left when you said 'stay',
If I was to have the time again
I'd have flown right back your way.

I love you Dad. Please be okay. I may
have settled afar but I still have not
gained the strength to walk this earth
without you.

See you soon,

Rose

Returning to Maggie Creek was nothing like Sasha had envisioned. A strong sense of calm clouded over her and she was not anxious at all. Jess collected her sister from the airport and very proudly escorted her home. It had been a long drive and as she drove past the front gates toward the main house, Sasha was in bliss. The land looked picturesque and all she could think was how she had never really appreciated its beauty before. Removing her dark sunglasses, Sasha's heart skipped a beat as the curve in the road exposed the old tin shed. Not a bad thought entered her head.

'No regrets' thought Sasha, as the winding road led them to the main house.

"He's a little more frail that you will remember" Jess said, trying to prepare Sasha for seeing Frank for the first time in so long.

"I won't lie. I'm a little scared that he won't have a clue who I am" shared Sasha, her voice shaking as she spoke.

Jess placed her hand in Sasha's and assured her that the disease was a slow one, and that in time he may become more forgetful but for now, he was okay. Still as grumpy and as gruff as ever.

As the sisters pulled up beside the old farmhouse, Sasha immediately spotted her father. He was standing outside leaning on his walking stick with their family home in the foreground.

'What an image' Sasha thought as she got out of the car and walked toward Frank. A few tears welled up in her eyes.

Sasha was happy to be back home, and even more happy to see her dad. He looked a little more wearier and she could see a few new wrinkles had appeared on his face and neck. As she wrapped her arms around Frank, she could feel he'd dropped a few kilos, but this was her dad. The one man in this world that loved her to no end.

"Ah, my Sash. You're home!" said Frank in his raspy voice, playing down the immense happiness he was feeling. As her tears began to fall, Frank pushed them away with his thumbs, cradling her face in his hands.

"Look at you my dear girl. We've missed you 'round

here" he said, ecstatic to see both his daughters in the one place.

By this time Jess was standing beside them and so Frank pulled both his daughters close, allowing his walking stick to fall. No words were needed. Frank was besotted with his girls and was so pleased to see them home.

The house appeared as it was when Sasha had left years before. Frank's old recliner still took pride of place on the old veranda just by the front door and as she walked inside, she wasn't surprised. Everything remained as it was years before, just as Frank liked it.

Walking through to the country kitchen, she could smell soup cooking in a big old heavy boiler.

"Is that what I think it is?" Sasha asked, pointing her question at Jess.

"Yes! It's Mum's secret soup" she replied whilst using a wooden spoon to stir the pot.

"Well I can't wait to sit down and devour a bowl for lunch."

That soup stood for family and the thought that Jess had prepared it for her homecoming made Sasha so grateful.

"This ain't lunch love. I have a surprise" chimed in Frank.

Unbeknown to Sasha and Jess, Frank had organised a big 'slap up' feast at the local pub on the edge of town.

"I wanna take my girls out for a nice meal"

announced Frank, who didn't usually do surprises.

"Dad, I'm tired. I appreciate the thought, but I really want to stay home and get some shut eye. I'm actually finding it odd that you of all people want to go out! What's got into you Dad?" she asked in jest.

Frank put his hand on Sasha's shoulder.

"We're goin' and that's final" he demanded, raising his eyebrows and lowering his voice.

Being lunchtime, the tiny local pub was almost full to the brim with patrons. The sounds of laughter and good times flowed through the open area with people sharing a yarn at the bar on the left and others seated waiting for their food on the right. With solid, dark beams across the tall pitched ceiling and a bold original fireplace in the corner, the pub was a welcoming waterhole. Its warmth coupled with the voices of happy children waiting for their lunches, created a homely feel and that's how Sasha felt when she'd walk through those doors. The smell of beer and country cooking wafted through the room. Fused with the scent of the old wooden floorboards, this truly was one of Sasha's favourite memories of home.

As she darted her eyes across the room, Sasha double backed. She took a short breath in, and looked directly at a man turning around to face her from the bar. It was James. 'Hot tin shed' James! Sasha's heart began to beat through her chest and the lively sounds from throughout the room dulled in her mind. They had not laid eyes on each other in so long although it did not feel like that to

Sasha. James had not changed at all, he was still the man she lusted after. Not time nor distance had taken those feelings away. With her eyes firmly glued to James, Sasha proceeded to walk over to greet him.

As she approached, he placed the tray of drinks he was carrying down onto a nearby table. Sasha awkwardly lent in for a friendly embrace and James reciprocated. He was clearly nervous, yet thrilled to see her. James' warmth radiated from his body and for a brief moment, she could feel his breath brush past her neck as he kissed her on the cheek. Sasha's brief fling with James was on her mind and that feeling, that yearning to feel his warmth again was still there. Even a momentary touch was enough to excite Sasha. She was so attracted to James that if they were not standing in a bar, Sasha would have been tempted to stretch that moment out. The nervous energy between them was obvious; obvious to the woman sitting at the table where James had placed the drink tray.

"Uh, Sash, I'm sorry. I'm being rude. This is my fiancé, Brielle. Brielle meet Sasha. She's Frank's daughter."

'Fuck… Fuck, fuck fuck fuck! Brielle is gorgeous. Gorgeous name, gorgeous body, gorgeous hair… Gorgeous, gorgeous, fucking gorgeous!' thought Sasha, who was quick to judge.

To Brielle's right sat a little boy with the most beautiful hazel eyes. Dylan had grown up into a boy with a lot of spunk. He was playing with a couple of cars on the table, kicking his legs and being boisterous.

"Join us" said Brielle, pulling a chair out and welcoming Sasha.

So down she sat, next to her new arch nemesis, or so Sasha thought. Her thinking was not so reasonable at that moment yet still she politely chatted for with Brielle. She of course greeted Dylan with a story or two from the past. James and Sasha barely spoke to each other as the conversation was led mostly by Brielle who wanted to know all about her fiancé's blast from the past.

"So, you've known James since school?" Brielle asked, with her perfect smile and perfect teeth on display.

"Yes, we've been friends a long time" answered Sasha, feeling particularly awkward.

Remnants of their lust for one and other still remained. There was a feeling between the two that still drew them together. James could barely take his eyes off Sasha. It was almost like not a day had passed since their steamy rendezvous in the tin shed that hot, summer night. Sasha's heart was still pounding and with her short sentences came a sense of awkwardness at the table.

As Sasha stood to get back to her family, James rose as well. She looked at him and he stared back. It briefly felt like the old days until Brielle chimed in.

"We will have to have you over for dinner while you're here!"

Sasha peered down at Brielle and Dylan, who was totally lost in play.

"I'm home for a month, I think. I'm sure I'll see you

around" she said, looking back up to face James.

"Yeah" he responded, nodding his head and clearly feeling uncomfortable.

Sasha took a breath before departing the table. As she walked away, Sasha noticed something. She no longer had those butterflies and although she was attracted to James, she was done. And at that very moment, as she smiled and greeted another old friend who was standing by the bar, she realised that whatever void he once filled was already full and that Sasha had filled it herself. She was fierce and ready to get back to being that independent, strong woman her mother saw within her; the woman she should have been all along.

CHAPTER TWENTY-FIVE

The Photograph

So here I am. Living in the moment.
Chasing nothing but my dreams,
running from no one. Grateful for every
moment I have.

My relationship with J is now just a
memory, a time when my decisions took
me to places I never thought I'd visit. I
was down, buried deep in a pit of denial
for so long. It's taken me years to feel like
I deserved to move forward and as I sit
here in my childhood bedroom, back
where I made such mistakes, I'm solemn.
And I own them.

Feeling happy to be home,

Rose

T he sun was shining brightly through the old style lace curtain that adorned the living room window. It was a hot January day and with Frank's fan blowing on her face, Sasha sat back in her father's cosy chair. With her laptop snuggly on her lap, she had begun to channel her inner Rafael and had planned to write. She told herself that it didn't matter if it made sense, and that with practice her words would begin to flow. And they were, slowly. Just as the hot Spanish guy had predicted.

Sasha never felt like she had enough time to write, when in reality, she had been so bogged down with the past, that fulfilling this part of herself had become a distant last place. Sure, Sasha kept up with her journal entries though free writing was a fairly new phenomenon in her eyes. She had the intention, just not the focus. It was a few days into her visit and Sasha had still managed to avoid James, and any talk of her mistakes.

So, she typed. And typed. Until she had spilled out one thousand words. It was quicker to type rather than use scraps of paper. Though Sasha preferred the old method when it came to her journal.

Lost in thought, Sasha continued to write. Her words began flowing out easier, and she was developing some good ideas for her novel. She had finally decided to take the plunge and it was this day that 'Rose' officially was awarded the lead who in some ways, had really been acting as the main character all along.

Suddenly without warning, Sasha heard a scream from out in the garden.

"Jess?" she exclaimed, recognizing her sister's voice. Sitting her laptop onto the table to the side of Frank's chair, Sasha raced outside to find her sister.

Over by Frank's vegetable patch, she could see Jess waving her arms.

"It's Dad! Quick! Call an ambulance!" shouted Jess, signalling that their father was hurt.

As quick as her legs could take her, Sasha ran into the kitchen to call for help. Her hands shook with fear and worry, as she dialled the emergency number. Peering out through the window, she could see Jess on her knees in a panic. As soon as she had gotten through to a real person and relayed the emergency, Sasha threw the phone down. As she raced out to see her father, the phone cord fell, swinging the handset from side to side. Frank was alert yet Sasha could see he had quite the injury.

"Sash, he's had a fall. He slipped and fell, bumping his head on this post" explained Jess, pointing toward the tree stump to the right of them.

Blood had been pouring from Frank's head wound, and a basket of freshly picked vegetables had fallen onto the ground. Jess had used Frank's over shirt in an attempt to stem the bleeding. It broke Sasha to see her father like this. Her once strong and capable father was becoming weak, and there was not one thing either sister could do about it.

Shortly an ambulance arrived to take Frank into the hospital. He demanded that both his daughters remain home.

"I'll be a while" he said, as the paramedics wheeled him toward the ambulance.

"But Dad!" Jess pouted.

"No, I said stay home. I'll get 'em to call you when they're done stitching me up."

Frank was serious. He wanted nothing more than to minimise the fuss and when news came in later that Frank was just fine, both Sasha and Jess were obviously relieved. They were also happy to hear that Dr. Stone had organised for Frank to spend the night for observation.

So, with this news, Sasha decided to pick up where

she left off, re-opening her laptop. She got comfy again, relaxing in Frank's big old chair and there she remained for an hour, lost in thought.

In the morning, she rose early and retreated to the comfort of Frank's chair. With a cup of tea in hand, she sat, staring at the screen, imagining what she'd write today. The steam wafting from her cup relaxed her, just as much as every delicate sip.

"Sasha!"

Calling her name from another room was Jess.

"Sash! Are you busy?"

As she closed her laptop, Sasha responded.

"I'm coming!"

She then found her sister who was about to tackle the mammoth task that was organising Frank's study.

"Are you sure he'd want us in here?" Sasha asked, wondering whether this was all a good idea.

The dust was thick in Frank's study as he obviously hadn't even opened the door in some time. As Sasha drew the curtains, a beam of light from the glistening morning sun shone on the vintage leather topped desk. Along one wall stood towering built in bookshelves, full of old books and even dusty trophies from when Frank competed in the local cricket club some 20 years prior. This room breathed Frank. It was a direct replication of who Frank was. Pictures of livestock on one side and an old photo of a race horse owned by his father before him, sat in its place, in the centre of the wall one would see when entering Frank's study. The walls themselves were a dark walnut colour and although dust covered every corner of the room, Sasha had fond memories of this old space. She remembered running in and seeing her father sitting at the desk, his dark framed glasses balancing on the tip of his nose.

"You start with this pile of papers and I'll start organising his drawers. Does that sound like a plan?" Jess asked.

"Sure. Let's do this!"

Sasha began to sift through the myriad old documents that littered Frank's desk. There was everything from old invoices to notes pertaining to farm business, from back when the farm was much more successful. These days, since James had left, no farm manager had really been taking care of Maggie Creek. Just the odd farm hand or two over the years.

"Is this you Sash? Because it sure ain't me!" Jess commented, holding up an old photograph.

Sasha squinted slightly as she analysed the photo. In it was a baby girl not much older than a few months old. As she stepped closer toward Jess, Sasha noticed the baby's distinctive hazel eyes.

"Hazel eyes" she said out loud.

And then she realised who the baby was in the photograph. A look of pure shock and confusion formed her expression. Sasha in that moment could have been knocked over by a feather.

"That's not me. But I know who it is."

It was like time had paused so that Sasha could take a

breath and gather her thoughts.

"It's Claire" she continued, sliding the photo from Jess' fingertips.

"Why would Dad have a photo of Claire as a baby? How odd!" Jess said, riding the same wave of confusion.

Sasha stared at the image as a barrage of memories came flooding in. The photograph was a duplicate of the one Claire had shown her all those years before. She recalled conversations with her friend, about how her father wasn't in her life.

Shaking, and unsure whether unearthing this theory was the right decision, Sasha chose to speak anyway.

"I think Claire..."

She stopped to clear her throat.

"I think Claire was Dad's daughter too."

With that, Jess fell into her father's office chair.

"No, how could that be?" Jess questioned, not understanding as to how Sasha could think such a thing.

Shock reigned as Jess got up to walk outside. Sasha didn't want to be right but her gut was telling her that she was. Their father, this upstanding, honest and wonderful man. The love of their mother's life; fathered another woman's baby.

Sasha needed more than this photo. So, after placing the photo into her pocket, she proceeded to dig through Frank's drawers. When that uncovered nothing but a few news clippings and more old invoices, she turned to the wall of bookshelves. Opening box after box, it wasn't long until Sasha found something that interested her.

Her mother's journals. She always knew they existed,

but never once thought to look for them in here. Finding her mother's diary in Frank's office.

One thing her mother was never short of was a story and she had this incredible ability to remember the finer details, the dates and other important information. Yet still, Sasha felt as if she was unearthing this whole other side to her mother. Reluctant yet naturally curious, she Sasha began to peruse the pages of her mother's journals. She could not believe that her mother had hid this side of herself. Her words were so finely put together.

'She could have been an author, my mum' Sasha pondered as she turned each page.

Sasha would not read every word however, as she browsed each book, she found little words of wisdom that danced their way into Sasha's heart.

Until she found the words Sasha would grow to dread.

"She knew" whispered Sasha.

A shudder ran down her spine. Her mother's haunting words were unbelievable, powerful and utterly devastating all at the same time. Maggie knew about Frank's affair, and furthermore, knew about Claire.

'How could she keep this to herself?'

Sasha pondered in amazement, her fingers just feathering across her mouth in shock. She swallowed, and took a deep breath before turning the next page. There she found something that made sense.

'Frank has hurt me deeply, so deep that I feel I cannot stay. Yet, leaving him is not an option. I take my vows seriously. I have Jessica and we have one more bundle of love on the way. How he could do this, I will never understand. Frank now has two new babies about to be born, and one of them is not mine. His apologies right now are falling on deaf ears. Though I forgive him and that is my choice. We are all flawed in some way and that does not mean we don't deserve forgiveness. For if we never forgave, no one on the earth would have anyone.'

Sasha sat there stunned for a moment, trying to absorb the myriad of truths that lay before her. She would go onto skim the remainder of journal number one that evening before placing the leather-bound book back into the box and sliding it deep under her bed.

Frank was to return home sometime in the afternoon. Both sisters decided it best they say nothing until the time was right. As best they could, Sasha and Jess erased all evidence that linked them from stepping foot in Frank's study. They drove to the local hospital, picked up their father and returned home. Frank was fine, just a little disorientated from all the drama.

The next morning, Sasha lay there, after just a few hours' sleep. She had dedicated her late night and early morning hours to learning more about her mother. She never once realised that her mum lived with such pain buried deep inside her. Sasha would have never known, if her mother hadn't died tragically, at a time when she was still young enough to live a good life. Sasha would have given up the privilege of knowing all she knew now, just to have her mother back; just to bring back the good old, oblivious days that was life on the farm. Lying in her single, childhood bed, she found listening to the birds chirping outside, a calming distraction. Sasha needed this moment, to come down off the painful roller coaster that she and Jess had experienced the night before. Reading her mother's first journal meant that Sasha was taking on the burdens that lie within it. Her mother was so deeply hurt yet stayed for Jess and Sasha. She compromised herself so that they could have the 'normal' life they grew accustomed to.

As Sasha reflected, she again, just like Rafael taught her to, she escaped without actually going anywhere. Reaching that La Gomera beach again was just the spiritual reprieve Sasha needed to put everything into perspective.

Despite meditating, she realised that it was inevitable. Sasha would have to wake back up and face the truth. The thought that her mother deserved to be treated better consumed Sasha. As she lay there, angry, unable to process how her father would do such a terrible thing to their family. The coldness that she felt toward her father shivered down her spine. He wasn't the man she thought he was. Yet, as the sun rose that morning, it dawned on Sasha that her mother had her reasons to stay.

Maggie believed in forgiveness and second chances. She was right when she wrote that we are all flawed in some way. Sasha knew very well that she too had made mistakes; mistakes like her father before her.

Suddenly she recalled that Claire in the end, was another version of Maggie. James was just another Frank. The thought that Sasha had hurt Claire so much – even if she wasn't aware before her death, was sickening. Reading her mother's journal was as much a learning process as it was personal.

History had repeated itself. And Sasha had played a starring role.

CHAPTER TWENTY-SIX

No Longer Just a Friend

The truth is, I can't judge him. For I was
once a sinner as well.

I never thought we were so alike

A chip off the old block,

Rose

Sasha couldn't let it go, and no matter how many times she brought her mind back to that luscious, sandy beach, she knew there was only one way out of this. Sasha and Jess had to become brave. They needed to confront Frank and it was important they do it soon. There would come a day when Frank wouldn't be able to recall such detail and the thought of this terrified Sasha.

As another day ended, Sasha grappled with the thought that Frank had this whole other life. Further to the point, Sasha too, had a history that involved Frank's illegitimate love child. Jess had no clue. She was pressuring Sasha, telling her that they needed to confront Frank.

"What if it's not true and we let this sordid rumour

fester?" she'd say, reminding Sasha that time was not on their side.

This went on for days, with no agreed solution in sight.

Peeling back her bed covers that next morning after another sleepless night, Sasha still had no idea about how she and Jess should go onto to tackle their dilemma. Approach him, perhaps, they thought. Or ignore. Though ignoring would be torture for both women. Because as Jess kept repeating, they simply had no time to waste.

Still not completely convinced and hoping for a reasonable explanation, Sasha built this story in her head, trying to suggest that the photo was just similar, that Claire's photo wasn't as she remembered. Briefly, she felt convinced that it couldn't be, yet still an element of doubt remained.

As she showered that morning, and as the soap from her shampoo trickled down the curves of her lean frame, she found herself lost in thought. He had to be Claire's father. Sasha had no doubt; despite endlessly wishing that she was wrong.

After dressing, she wrapped a towel around her head and strolled out into the living room. There was Jess, just finishing off a video call with Ally and Eliza.

"Oh, I miss them, Sash. I really can't wait to go home. Do you think you could handle things here for a week? I'll come back. I just miss Ally and Eliza so much."

Without a second thought, Sasha comforted her

sister.

"Of course! You go. Seriously, I've got this" she explained.

"But first, let's talk to Dad. I think it's time" Sasha whispered to Jess.

This is one issue that the pair were beginning to disagree on. Although on board in the beginning, Jess no longer wanted to speak with Frank about it. She felt that the very idea that Claire was their sister was fresh out of a daytime soap, and Sasha hadn't yet shared their mother's journals with her sister. She simply didn't want to do it until she was positive. Yet facing the facts, Sasha knew the truth. It was written in her mother's books. She just didn't want to believe it.

"Sasha, I'm not doing this. You have no facts and you're going to go in and say something so outlandish that Dad is going to laugh in your face!"

Jess was serious. She had figured it all out. The man she knew as her father wouldn't do this. She was convinced.

Sasha stood there defiant.

"No. I'm doing it. I want him to tell me why he kept Claire a secret from us" she said, quietly yet abruptly before marching into see her father.

As she walked out of the room, she tossed her towel over the arm of the small settee that had been in the hallway for years and continued into the kitchen. Jess called out and said she was going into town, not wanting to be around for the potential explosion that was likely to ignite between Sasha and Frank.

There he was, standing across from Sasha in the kitchen of the old farm house. She could sense that he knew there was something on her mind. This was going to be the hardest conversation Sasha would ever have with her father. She took two steps forward and took a silent breath in. With her hand shaking, she placed the photo of Claire on the island bench.

"Explain to me how a photo of Claire as a baby got into your drawer" she said, fearful of his imminent reaction.

Her father stood there, glaring at the picture sitting in front of him. Sasha could see that Frank's eyes had turned glassy and as he blinked, single tears trickled out. He swallowed, and gasped, covering his mouth with his right hand. He took a step back, toward the sink behind him and shook his head.

"How did you get this? Have you been goin' through my things?"

Sasha replied, shaking yet still quite stern.

"Is Claire your daughter?

She took another breath and continued.

"My sister?"

Frank cleared his throat with a grunt and paused for a moment. The tension in the room built, as the truth was about to reluctantly be exposed. Sasha knew she had backed her father into a corner. There was no way he could deny it. Feeling an innate sense of disappointment, she pounced on him.

"Why Dad?! Why did you do this? How could you do this?" she said, whilst pounding his chest.

"You lied to us! You lied to Mum! How could you?!" she screamed, in a fit of anger.

Frank grabbed hold of his daughter's arms, attempting to calm her.

"Sasha, stop! Just stop! It's true. Claire was my daughter" he confessed, no longer fighting back his tears.

Struggling out from his unwanted embrace, Sasha shoved her father into the kitchen bench beyond and looked frantically around the room.

Unable to handle another moment in this emotion filled room, Sasha tried to flee, until Frank stopped her with these fateful words.

"Your mother knew" he said, sharing a bombshell that Sasha did not expect him to confess.

She stopped. Facing away from her father. With her heart racing, she turned and looked at him. Frank was frail, he appeared beaten, as if he had been holding it together for so long, only to feel deflated when he was able to release it.

"She knew?" questioned Sasha, acting oblivious.

"Yes" Frank responded.

Frank's decision to bring her mother into this whirlwind was too much for Sasha.

'How dare he' she thought, before looking down at her feet.

Here was her father, a man she trusted and adored; a man she idolised. Then there was the memory of her mother; a woman with the patience and loyalty of a saint.

"I don't even know you" Sasha said to her upset father.

"Well it's true" he said.

"I did something that I'm far from proud of and it meant nothin'. You girls, your mother. I let you all down."

As the tears continued to fall down her cheeks, she gritted her teeth.

"Claire meant something" she choked, barely able to express her words.

"She meant something the day that she was born."

Memories started flowing back, such as when she learned of Claire's illness. Her father knew before James had said anything.

Frank limped toward Sasha, attempting to comfort her; or reason with her. She didn't want that. In fact, the last person Sasha felt comfort from right now was her father. She shook her head in disgust, feeling like she wanted to be sick. He wasn't who she thought he was, and there was no going back from this moment. Their relationship was to never be the same again.

As Sasha left Frank in the kitchen, she went to her room and cried. She cried a million tears; for her father,

her mother and for her sister, Claire. It was in this moment that she reminded herself that not only Frank had let Claire down, Sasha had as well. Devastated, she began to pack her things.

"This is not my home anymore. I don't belong here" she said to herself.

Then that old wave of guilt came into play again.

'Running would achieve nothing' Sasha thought before removing the clothes she had stuffed into her well-travelled suitcase.

Claire was no longer just a friend; she was blood. Even though her father had just lost his crown, Sasha realised that she had lost her own only years before.

Frank wasn't the only one to let Claire down.

CHAPTER TWENTY-SEVEN

Surprise

I sit here alone, under my favourite apple tree. It's not the prettiest nor is it the tallest. And it certainly doesn't shade the sun from my eyes. With broken branches and its remnants laying stagnant on the ground, it's not as robust as it used to be.

At least my favourite tree is still here and for as long as it stands upright and strong, I will continue to admire it for all it has given me.

Rose

Another few weeks had passed and Jess had finally arrived back at the farm. She was away a little longer than expected and came back with a proposition for Sasha and Frank. Before Jess left, Frank had told her the truth about Claire. Jess oddly took it better than anybody expected although a longer break from the farm helped.

"Dad, Sash. I want to run something by you" she said, clutching a ladle as she dished up tonight's curry.

"Spit it out darl" said Frank, noticing that Jess was nervous, spilling curry sauce all over the bench.

"You know how things are changing around here

and you're going to need some help? Well. Sasha will be going back to England soon."

Frank's expression didn't change. He sat listening intently and snacking on nuts from a bowl on the dining table.

"Yes?" he questioned, waiting for Jess to indeed 'spit it out'.

"Well, it got me thinking. What if Ally, Eliza and I came and lived in the cottage."

Frank lent back into his chair, placing his hands behind the back of his head. He didn't look all that impressed by Jess' proposal.

"No. You've told me over and over how much you like it up north. I'm not havin' you all turn your lives upside down because of me. I just won't have it!"

Frank was serious, shaking his head back and forth.

"Dad, like it or not you need us around. I'm telling you, this is best for everyone. Ally and I want to live down here and for Eliza to grow up on the farm well, I couldn't think of a better place to raise her."

This all sounded logical to Sasha who had been secretly fearing she'd have to throw away her life overseas. She had daydreamed about having to trade it in for the farm all over again and it just wasn't what she wanted.

"Please just agree Dad" Jess begged, whilst Sasha remained quiet.

"I said no. Are you not listenin' to me?"

Frank was not in the mood to compromise and as Sasha dished up his curry with a side of rice, he got up out of his chair and hobbled over to collect it.

His silent disapproval didn't deter Jess who had already made plans. She was moving to the farm whether he was happy about it or not.

That night after Frank had retired to bed, the two sisters chatted about Jess' plans to uproot her family.

"I'm telling you, Ally is on board. She even suggested it. We just want to be around to makes sure he looks after himself" Jess said, further convincing Sasha that this was the ideal scenario for everyone.

Sasha agree, nodding her head with a smile.

"Only one more week until I'm heading back" Sasha commented.

She scanned her eyes around the room looking at the familiar objects that made this old house a home.

"I'm going to miss the farm, and of course you. And Dad" she said.

"But at least we have the internet for video calls. I want to watch Eliza grow. She's going to be a lucky girl growing up here."

Interrupted by a notification sound on her laptop that was sitting idle on her lap, Sasha looked to see what it was.

"Oh, sorry Jess. I've... I've got a call" she stammered, before quickly running to her room, with her laptop out in front of her.

Sitting down on her bed, Sasha was shocked to see Keir video calling her. It had been quite some time since they had exchanged messages.

After fluffing her hair with her fingers, she pushed the green button.

"Hi!" said Sasha, with excitement.

Keir looked happy to see her too. He greeted her and as he did, Keir panned his camera to show off his surroundings.

"Surprise! Look where I am!" he said in his very British accent.

She knew exactly where he was.

"You're outside Cruz Magazine? In London?! Are you mad?" she answered with surprise.

"Come down!" Keir instructed, clearly in an effort to come off as spontaneous.

"I don't know how to tell you this but I'm not in England. I'm back in Australia on my Dad's farm."

As he heard her words, disappointment filtered through his expression.

"I'm sorry. We haven't spoken in a while and this visit was as much a surprise to you as it was for me. Why are you in England? I really hope you didn't make a special trip to see me!"

Standing on the busy street, he explained he had to go. Once he made it to his hotel, Keir promised to message Sasha and explain everything.

For the next hour, she waited patiently to hear from Keir and when the time come, he gave her a call.

"I really wanted to surprise you with this news" Keir said, much less excited than before.

"Oh Keir, you've surprised me already. That's for sure!" Sasha quipped.

He laughed.

"I have actually accepted a job over here. I'm in the midst of relocating to London."

Luckily Sasha was sitting down. Never did she see that coming.

"Wow! Well, I'm coming back shortly. We'll have to catch up."

The old flames chatted for hours, mostly about Sasha and how her family had been turned upside down. Then without thought, she let it all go. Sasha told Keir about everything. Her father's affair, Claire, her time in Spain with Rafael and her biggest secret of all, her affair with James.

Keir blamed himself.

"You wouldn't have had to go through all of that if I wasn't such a mess back then. Sasha, I let you down. I'm so truly sorry for that."

"You've already apologised months ago."

Keir shook his head.

"I didn't know you had been through such pain after I left you that night. Not only did you lose your mother, you lost your way. I'm genuinely sorry for what I put you through. Let me make it up to you."

Sasha and Keir decided that he would be there to greet her as she got off the plane from Australia.

And with that, something old but new had begun all over again. Sasha had pushed reset on her relationship with Keir.

CHAPTER TWENTY-EIGHT

Romancing with the Past

Flirting with the unknown
Toying with the past, I blush,
For I never imagined in my wildest
dreams you could give me such a rush.

See you when I land,

Rose

S tepping off the plane and into the airport, Sasha was excited to be home. She would miss her family, despite the madness that had went down during her month-long visit. Feeling inspired, Sasha had spent the entire flight writing and by this point, her novel was half complete. Everything was looking up for Sasha. All at Maggie Creek had settled down, she had made some serious strides with her book and she was about to walk into the loving arms of Keir; the man she had grown to love once more.

Letting her imagination run away with her, Sasha imagined him; standing there waiting anxiously for her arrival. She pictured him back before the demise of their relationship. That charming older man with the equally charming English accent. Oh, how Sasha used to love listening to Keir for hours, long into the night. She hoped they still had that chemistry, that elusive spark, and as she walked through the last gate, now with her luggage in toe, that moment made it abundantly clear.

There was her prince charming, as handsome and as dapper as ever.

She stood still for a second and admired the view. He was dressed as he always was; suit and tie, but with a welcoming addition. The most glorious bunch of white roses Sasha had seen in a long time.

As they walked towards each other, that chemistry she remembered became stronger and as if not a day had gone by since their rendezvous' in Australia, he pulled Sasha in, hugging her tight.

"Oh, how I've missed you Sash" he said before their embrace became something straight out of the movies.

Sharing a kiss that lingered longer than her imagination could predict, the couple then walked hand in hand until they reached a place to sit. Sasha and Keir talked for an hour before he escorted her back to her apartment.

"I won't come up. I'll let you rest. Let's see each other tomorrow" he said, before kissing Sasha on the cheek.

Sasha was besotted with just how romantic he was. Remnants of the good times re-entered her mind as she unlocked the door of her flat. Sasha's little bolt hole in

London was just as she left it, outdated beige scatter cushions and all.

The next day came and just like the last, it was magical. Like a fairy-tale. Sasha and Keir had come full circle, as if it was fate that pulled them back together.

As her life began to adjust to its new normal, Sasha returned to work with Vee. Cruz Magazine hadn't changed all that much and Freya was pleased to make her way back into the Writer's Department. Vee promised Sasha that her job would be waiting and she came through on her promise.

Keir had begun working at a major London hospital and had soon moved from his luxury hotel into Sasha's tiny abode. The couple were blissfully happy, enjoying a similar social life as they had all those years ago in Australia. The only difference is that they were older. Sasha's career was set to boom and the pair were making plans. Big plans. Sasha couldn't imagine spending her life with any other man.

"Darling, fetch me that Portman file" ordered Vee, as she sat her bony behind on the corner of Sasha's desk.

"While you do that, why not fill me in on where you've been lately? How is life in the love nest? A.k.a, your former bachelorette pad."

Vee's questions were met with a discerning look from Sasha.

"I know you're not keen on Keir. You can just say it!" she responded, unpleased that Vee couldn't just be happy for her.

"Oh, you mean the foolish little man who left you stranded in the street? I bet you wish you never told me about him! Someone once told me I have the memory of an elephant, and thankfully not the body of one. But my point is, are you sure you can really trust the snake?"

Vee's words made Sasha cross.

"Seriously Vee, keep it up and you'll not only be losing an assistant. You'll be losing a friend!"

Sasha meant business. All she wanted was her friend to be supportive. She was in love, deep love and nothing Vee could say would change her mind.

"Okay, I'm sorry. Let me take you both out for dinner. My treat. He'll schmooze me and I'll schmooze back. We'll be a happy little friendship of three in no time at all."

Vee smirked as she stood up to walk away.

Sasha dreaded the day that Vee and Keir made it to the same room. She just knew it wouldn't end well.

Out of the corner of her eye, Sasha noticed another familiar face. It was Stan, the not-so-good-looking boss of the one and only Rafael.

"Stan!" she called.

"Oh Sasha! Nice to see you back!" he responded, like her long, lost buddy.

After a few moments of small talk, this led to Sasha taking the plunge and asking after Rafael. She was disappointed to hear that he had moved on, but when

Stan explained that he'd just published his first novel, Sasha was enamoured. She made it a point to stop by that bookshop where they met to find if it was on sale.

"What is his book called?" she asked with anticipation.

"Oh, I have it. Let me just get my copy from my desk."

Stan toddled and soon returned, handing his soft cover copy to Sasha. As she held it with her fingertips, Sasha was blown away at what she saw.

"Hey, now I see it, that looks like you!" Stan commented, pointing to the sketched cover, a woman with her eyes closed, lost in thought.

And the title? 'Niña perdida.'

Sasha politely handed back the book and waved goodbye to Stan who was heading out for lunch.

As he strolled away, she quickly typed the words 'Niña perdida' into an online translator.

"Little Girl Lost" she read out loud, realising that Rafael's book was based on her.

Now getting her hands on a copy was even more important to Sasha.

'We only knew each other for a week! There's got to be some kind of mistake' she thought, whilst getting on with her work.

Nevertheless, Sasha would soon take her lunchbreak and head to the book store where she picked up a copy of 'Niña perdida' for herself.

That night whilst Keir was working, she began to read Rafael's book. She was right, most of it was pure fiction, but the main character well, she was certainly based on Sasha. Feeling quite proud to be secretly featured in Rafael's romance novel, she kept it to herself. Keir needn't know as her time in La Gomera was just a memory; a beautiful and uplifting memory.

CHAPTER TWENTY-NINE

Moving In

As I stare aimlessly above, I feel
captivated by their form, how they move
and how they shape together to create
the most wondrous display.

That's how I feel when I'm with you,
imagining our life together. The form our
future will take and the shapes we will
make together.

With all my love,

Rose

❝Sweetheart, can you meet me at my colleagues house at 6pm? I'll text you the address. That is so I don't have to come home before we go out for dinner" asked Keir, obviously in a rush.

Sasha was to join Keir for dinner with Dr. Swatsky and his wife. Evan Swatsky was Keir's supervisor at the hospital. Sasha hadn't yet had the privilege of meeting any of Keir's colleagues yet was excited by the prospect.

"Sure, just message me the address and I'll be there on time" she answered.

Sasha had planned to wear black so that the diamond earrings Keir had spoiled her with just days before, would be the star against her soft, tanned skin.

It was Saturday afternoon. She had spent the morning alone in her apartment, reading Rafael's novel. She could barely put it down as each chapter would bring a different memory of the time she spent in La Gomera.

Time was getting away from her and soon she had to get ready for her much-anticipated night out. As she slipped herself into her body hugging, mid-length dress, Sasha kept reflecting on how truly happy she had become. There was not a thing out of place in this life of hers, and she had to pinch herself just to ensure this all was indeed reality.

Once she made herself presentable, Sasha took a taxi ride to the address that Keir had sent her. Pulling the bottom of her dress down as she stood up after getting of the car, the enormous home in front of Sasha drew her eye up.

'Wow' she thought, whilst taking a moment to get her bearings. There stood before her was the most glorious old Victorian, with every desirable feature one could imagine.

Walking up the steps to the large and shiny, pitch black door, she darted her eyes from left to right. Beautiful and tall manicured trees framed the porch, and Juliet style balconies evened out the façade.

Sasha rang the doorbell, and soon heard footsteps approaching the entrance.

"Keir?" she said, as his familiar face answered the

door.

"Come in sweetheart" he said, with a smile.

"I hope you haven't been waiting too long" Sasha commented back, before stopping in her tracks.

In front of her was an almost palatial staircase. The parquet floor would have been original and smell of the wood permeated the room. Stepping inside the front room Sasha was again overcome with its beauty. The large windows and feature ceilings captivated Sasha yet what was more puzzling was the fact that the house was empty.

"What is this?" she asked Keir, as he led her into the buildings dining room, lit with a countless array of candles and a fold out table for two in its centre.

Keir was beaming with excitement and quickly announced a surprise.

"I bought this house for us."

Sasha, taken aback had to catch her breath.

'Did I just hear that right?' she pondered, internally and as they dined that evening, just the two of them, it sunk into Sasha that this was real.

Her life had taken this unexpected turn and needless to say, she was in love. Nothing could make her happier than to live out her future in this house, with Keir by her side.

CHAPTER THIRTY

Blessed

I am in awe of this house. From its grand proportions to its large bay windows, flooding the house with light.
I have never stepped foot in a house where there is a marble fireplace in every room! Oh, how did I get here?

Still blissfully lost in love,

Rose

Waking from her short and uncomfortable slumber, Sasha sat up and got out of bed. She had lived in the enormous Victorian house for the past year and had relished every moment, from decorating to hosting dinners. From enjoying cosy nights in front of the fire to lazy Sunday mornings spent in bed with her love. She was living a blessed life.

The past nine months had been particularly special as Sasha had spent it pregnant. It had been a problem-free pregnancy, with nothing more than some relentless morning sickness. Yet in time that had passed, and the uncomfortable last months were all she had to get through before meeting their 'little bundle of love'.

Sasha had remembered that those were the words her mother had used to describe her. Those journals of her mother's still played an integral part in Sasha's life. Maggie had recorded so much of how she was feeling during her pregnancies and this helped ease Sasha's every concern.

As she showered and got dressed, Sasha felt that today would be the day that her baby would be born. Call it an innate sense of motherly intuition or a good dose of logic, but she knew.

An hour or two passed and those little twinges she was experiencing had turned to pain. They were intensifying, and with that she decided to call Keir who was already at work. Picking up the phone, she dialled his number. Shocked, yet pleased, he answered and immediately sent a car for Sasha. He met her at the hospital doors, where she was brought into the maternity department by wheelchair.

By this point, it was clear, she would most definitely be having her baby that day. Sasha's obstetrician explained to both she and Keir that baby's position wasn't ideal for birthing naturally, so they tossed their birth plan out the window and prepared for a caesarean.

Prepped and ready for surgery, Sasha was feeling nervous but okay. She was just anxious to hold her baby. Keir sat by her side the whole time, stroking her hair and whispering loving messages Sasha's way. His banter with the nursing staff helped relax Sasha as well. She felt safe, and with Keir clasping her hand, she felt the pull, of the painless cut.

It felt like just minutes had passed and Sasha heard the faintest, tiny cry. As the doctor held their baby up in the air, both Keir and Sasha looked on with delight. There she was. Their baby girl, healthy and full of life.

A short time later, Sasha was wheeled down from recovery, and had her first cuddle with her baby daughter.

"Oh, I love her" she said, with pure joy.

Keir was there, looking on with a beaming smile; clearly feeling the same kind of love.

"I already thought of a name, sweetheart. I do hope you like it" he said.

"Really?" Sasha said, puzzled by his confidence and curious to hear his choice.

"Stella Margaret Sterling. Stella because she is just so beautiful and Margaret, after your mother" he said, still smiling, with a twinkle in his eye.

Consumed with happiness and shedding a tear or two, Sasha was more in love with Keir than ever before. He had just given her a gift that she did not realise she wanted. A way to honour her mother. Sasha and Keir had discussed names during her pregnancy, yet never had they come up with such a fitting name.

"It is perfect, Keir. Thank you" cried Sasha, whilst she watched her man cradle their baby daughter in his arms.

Keir lent down and place Stella beside her mother on the bed. Sasha's gaze couldn't bear to look away from the beauty that was her daughter. She stared into Stella's little eyes and had something she felt compelled to share.

"You couldn't be more perfect Stella Margaret. May you have your grandmother's strength and your father's charm."

"And your mother's heart" continued Keir, as if this moment couldn't get any more special.

"Sasha, you have made me so happy, more than I ever thought I could be."

Keir looked in to Sasha's eyes, connecting on a level deeper than before. He didn't have to say a word. His face told her everything she wanted to know. He loved her just as much as she adored him. That's all Sasha craved; love and acceptance. So pure and real.

Behind Keir, appeared a familiar face. He turned and greeted the visitor.

"Jess! Oh, my goodness. What are you doing here?" gasped Sasha, realising what she was seeing was actually happening.

"Keir flew me in to help you during the last couple of weeks of your pregnancy. It seems you didn't need me after all!" she joked, as she spotted baby Stella.

Nothing else mattered more to Sasha than family and here she was, feeling more fortunate than ever before.

CHAPTER THIRTY-ONE

True Colours

As he unlocked the door and guided me inside with the palm of his hand, I felt safe. Like a fairy tale, our reception room looked like a scene out of one of the classics. Soft pink roses sat in place, illuminated by precisely strung fairy lights and soft music. A single note sat in front of the blooms and as I reached down to pick it up, he clasped my arm, rescuing the note from the tips of my fingers.

"Let me" he said softly, kneeling beside our precious daughter who lay sleeping in her capsule.

As he read the note, I felt tears well

in my eyes. Happy tears. The kind of tears every woman wants to feel run down her face.

He shared a tale of a man and a woman brought together by a floating piece of paper, bonded by curiosity and instant infatuation. I knew what was coming. A proposal to marry this extraordinary man. And I had my answer.

My answer was yes.

Smitten,

Rose

"Sshh, everybody! He is walking up to the front step!" Sasha said quietly, urging her guests to remain silent.

As Keir arrived home from work and walked through to the reception room, he was left astounded by the efforts Sasha had taken to help him celebrate his birthday.

"Surprise!" the room called before breaking into song.

Sasha stood in the centre of the room wearing a mint coloured dress and her mother's precious pearls. She was smiling and holding baby Stella on her hip who matched her mother from head to toe.

Keir walked over and kissed Sasha on the cheek, whispering words into her ear.

"You shouldn't have."

Sasha could sense he wasn't entirely pleased yet put his slight annoyance down to the fact he probably had a stressful day at the hospital.

What began a little dicey, turned into a lovely night. A selection of Keir's work colleagues attended along with Sasha's bestie, Vee who had all but moved on from her previous opinion of Keir.

As Keir chatted to his guests, Sasha spent most of her evening chatting with Vee.

It wasn't long and the last guest had left just before midnight. Sasha kicked off her shoes and approached Keir who was sitting quietly on a chair in front of the blazing fireplace.

Placing both hands on his shoulders, she began to massage them, paying special attention to Keir on his birthday. Almost straight away, he moved his body forward, urging Sasha to stop.

"If you think tonight was a good idea, you are sadly mistaken. Never embarrass me like that again" he said, in a stern tone.

Taking a step back, Sasha felt confused. The night had been wonderful, and she just couldn't understand Keir's extreme reaction.

"What are you talking about? You had fun tonight!" she exclaimed, trying to force her point.

"I don't like surprises, so I ask that you never do that again without my permission."

He was brutally straight to the point. Sasha began to see a side to Keir she hadn't seen before. She hoped that by the time tomorrow came around, that he would apologise for his harshness but that apology never came.

"And I don't think you should be going back to work at the magazine next month. We can't afford a nanny after all" he clamoured, before making his way upstairs in a huff.

Sasha couldn't quite believe what she was hearing and that night she chose to sleep in one of the guest bedrooms. She had no desire to lie next to Keir that night. He had just crushed her months of preparation and now he wanted her to quit her job.

There was an injustice going on and Sasha needed to get her head around it.

CHAPTER THIRTY-TWO

Don't Go Crushing My Heart

How does one just switch personalities
like that? Surely, he'll apologise and we
can put this night behind us.

Hurt and confused,

Rose

'Couples disagree' justified Sasha, as she woke the next morning. Her hair dishevelled and still wearing the mint green dress from the night before.

After leaving the guest bedroom next to Stella's room, she popped her head in to see her daughter sleeping soundly. Her satin white cot was like a frame, protecting the most important person in Sasha's life.

"I love you" she mouthed, kissing Stella gently and stroking her soft tuft of hair.

'She is my world' Sasha thought to herself as she tiptoed out of the room.

Opening the main bedroom door, she half expected

to see Keir dressing for work. Instead, just a lone note sat idle on her side of the bed.

'Pack a suitcase for you and Stella. I'm taking you both away for a few days.'

Sasha was expectedly surprised. After last night, this was the last thing she could have imagined. A surprise family trip.

'But to where?' she pondered.

She wouldn't know until Keir got home and by the sounds of the note, Sasha assumed he had been called into work on his day off.

Stepping into their grand scale ensuite, Sasha began to run a bath. As she waited, she stripped off last night's clothing, and sat on the side of the tub, testing the temperature with her toes. As the water rose, she slipped her body down into the ink coloured clawfoot bath. Whilst watching the water flow at her feet, Sasha realised that Keir must have known he was wrong and that this grand gesture of a trip away must have meant he was sorry. It didn't make it all okay, but to Sasha he was trying and that's all that mattered.

By the time her bath was over, baby Stella had woken. So, after dressing herself and changing the baby, Sasha made her way downstairs, knowing she had some work to do.

Utterly stunned, she was confronted with yet another surprise. The reception room where Keir's party was held had been cleaned from top to bottom! Not a single glass or crumb was in sight.

"Your Daddy is wonderful!" cheered Sasha, dancing baby Stella around the room.

To Sasha, these surprises meant that her Prince Charming had returned. She couldn't wait to see him and spent the morning feeding Stella and packing for their spontaneous few days away.

CHAPTER THIRTY-THREE

Just the Three of us

He may not enjoy surprises, but I do!

I do hope this is his way of saying sorry.

Blissfully happy,

Rose

They had drove north for hours through glorious English countryside to a chocolate box cottage in the middle of nowhere. It was pitch black outside, although the lanterns hanging beside the front door illuminated its façade.

"Oh, it's perfect!" said Sasha, as she carried Stella toward the entrance.

"I'm glad you like it" Keir said with smile as he pulled their luggage along behind him.

It truly was picture-perfect though seeing it was so late, there was no time to explore. Sasha placed her sleeping beauty down into a portable cot and the couple fell asleep almost instantly; a log burner keeping them toasty warm.

Waking from her slumber the next morning, Sasha opened her weary eyes to Keir sitting on the edge of the bed playing with Stella. Rubbing her eyes, Sasha noticed that her daughter had been dressed in the most beautiful lace dress, and she hadn't seen it before.

"Where did that come from?" she asked, touching the delicate gown with her fingers.

"I bought it for Stella. Do you like it?" Keir asked, with a grin.

A little shocked that Keir had been shopping for baby clothes, Sasha beamed.

"It's beautiful" she said, admiring the dresses fine, boho style.

Suddenly, Keir got up and placed Stella on his hip.

"Come with us. We have a surprise" he said, indicating that he wanted Sasha to join them downstairs.

"Another surprise?" she whispered, under her breath.

Putting her robe around her shoulders and walking slowly down the creaking stairs, Sasha began to hear sounds from what she imagined was an old-style music box. With each step, Keir's latest surprise was being exposed.

Reaching the bottom, a waft of sweet flora invaded Sasha's senses and her eyes began to be drawn to the beauty that filled the room.

As she continued to look around, she noticed that the space was filled with long stemmed, white roses, just like the ones Keir had gifted her at the airport all that time ago. Two oversized, cream armchairs sat close by a fireplace and a matching sofa lined a second wall. Particularly immense, classic oil paintings adorned the pure, white walls and a long, oak cabinet held what seemed to be family photographs and petite trinkets. Sasha glanced over toward a large window with a drapery of soft, cream coloured fabrics that elegantly dropped onto the floor. Just to the right of the window was a curve shaped structure and on second glance, Sasha realised it was indeed an archway threaded with hundreds of small, ashen blooms. The music box continued to play, giving the attractively decorated living room a slightly eerie feel.

As Sasha began to step further into the room, Keir stood there smiling.

"How was your sleep sweetheart?" he asked.

In awe and totally lost in the moment, Sasha answered describing her sleep, and the room as total magic.

"What is all of this?" she asked, before kissing her two loves gently on their cheeks.

After placing Stella into Sasha's arms, Keir indicated with just his finger and the excitement written all over his face, that there was yet another thing he hadn't told her about.

"I have been saving this for you" he said whilst

unzipping a clothing bag that was draped across one of the oversized armchairs.

What he revealed was the biggest shock of all. There lay one of the most elegant, lace wedding gowns Sasha had ever seen.

"I've pictured you in this so many times, and now that the day has come. We can have the wedding we've always dreamed about" explained Keir, still beaming from ear to ear.

Sasha was slightly bewildered by Keir's gesture. It was the most grand and romantic gesture yet, though Sasha couldn't help but feel that this was a little strange. Sure, they had discussed getting married, though here they were, in some cottage in the middle of nowhere. There was no family, friends, nor somebody here to officiate the nuptials.

Something just didn't seem right.

"Keir, as much as I appreciate all of your effort and it is so very lovely" Sasha continued, trying to understand how this was all going to play out.

"I'm just not sure this is what we talked about. I mean, I don't want to sound ungrateful but I always imagined we would do this back on my family farm. You know, how we talked about it."

Keir came close to Sasha and kissed her gently on her forehead.

"Put the dress on, and this will all make sense soon" he said, leaving a lot to Sasha's imagination.

At once, he took baby Stella and skilfully pulled the floral arch out through the small front door.

"Are you right with that?" Sasha asked, politely yet still trying to figure out what on earth was going on.

"I've got it, you just get dressed" Keir answered, closing the door behind him.

As the bride-to-be started to hesitantly undress, she decided to live in the moment. This all didn't seem quite right but she figured she would soon know what was going on.

Sasha carefully stepped into the gown, lifted it up over her bust and struggled to fasten the garment at the back. Soon she was dressed and waiting for Keir to return. Noticing that he had thought of everything, she ran a brush through her hair and pinned it up, opting to lose the bed hair look before Keir returned. Opening her beauty bag that was conveniently in its place in the downstairs bathroom, she swiftly applied some make up.

While waiting, Sasha spent time exploring the intricacies of the room. She admired the light, floral arrangements and the oversized paintings of female figures. The mantelpiece above the open fire was polished a marbled white and a large, ceiling height mirror hung brilliantly above. On top of the cabinet sat a small photo frame surrounded by little ornaments and crystal sculptures. Sasha glanced casually at the photograph and was stunned by what she saw. There was Keir with his arms wrapped around another woman.

Then it dawned on her.

'Was that Matilda?' she wondered.

As Sasha tried very hard to cast her mind back to that day in the park, that day they met. When she laid eyes on the photo that had blown her way.

"Oh my god..." Sasha whispered, cupping her mouth with her hands.

Before she could say another word, Keir re-entered the room. Dressed in a dark coloured, pin stripe suit, finished with a white lily button hole, his cheerful smile did it's best to light up the room. A wave of emotions ran through her mind as he approached her.

"Who is this?" Sasha asked forwardly, holding up the photo frame.

Keir expression turned glum.

"That was taken before" he paused.

"Before what?" asked the now not so blushing bride.

"Before Matilda died" he said, looking down at his feet.

"You're standing in my childhood home. I know it's not Australia but I do hope you'll forgive me once you see what I have prepared for you. I've been planning this day since the moment we brought Stella home."

His words certainly captured Sasha's attention as she noticed that Stella wasn't with him. She walked eagerly toward the door and as she opened it, her concerns just faded away.

In the distance under a big old tree, stood those who mattered most to Sasha; Jess with Eliza safely on her hip. Ally was standing there too, holding their daughter's hand. And what was perhaps the most astonishing gift of all, there was Frank, sitting comfortably on an old wooden bench.

Sasha could have passed out. This was all so much to

take in. Never would she have pictured this and for the life of her, she couldn't figure out how this fiancé of hers could continually pull theses surprises off in such a succession.

Not only their wedding day, it was a reunion. Her father was able to meet his new granddaughter and Sasha could hug him tight. Frank had aged quite a bit and as his daughter, Sasha knew that coming all the way to England would have been quite a feat for her farm-loving dad.

Shortly, after embracing each of her family, it was time to marry her love. At the beautifully detailed arch stood a woman who was ready to officiate their nuptials.

As Sasha began to walk slowly towards Keir, her heart fluttered with pure joy and anticipation. Her graceful, floor length, lace gown flowed elegantly as she progressed towards him. She watched as Keir's face lit up in awe as he reached out to touch her hands.

Keir paused.

"You are beautiful, just like a princess. I'm so fortunate to have you in my life" he said in a softly spoken manner.

The sound of the music box also placed at the arch had in time slowed down and as Keir and Sasha stared into each other's eyes, time felt still.

As the music stopped, they committed themselves to each other, reading the classic vows and kissing to seal their marriage.

Reaching over to turn the dial just one more time, Keir started the soft music all over again. Placing his arms around Sasha's waist and gently edging her closer, he kissed her on the neck. She could feel his breath on her body as he leant down to hug her, planting his lips on her neck just one more time. They danced briefly as their guests gushed in envy.

Soon the music had stopped and Sasha could hear only the beat of Keir's heart as she buried her head into his chest.

The husband and wife danced slowly, swaying from side to side for some time, enjoying the feeling of closeness. All the while, Sasha's thoughts had reached a new intensity. This man of hers couldn't be any more perfect, she thought, raising her head up to face her family.

"Sasha, let's take Stella to Australia. We can do this all over again, just as we had planned."

Keir's words brought Sasha's attention back to her husband.

"Yes!" she said, beaming from ear to ear.

And that is what they did, spending a few weeks back on the farm together and in love.

CHAPTER THIRTY-FOUR

A Quiet New Life

It's been some time since I've seen you. Felt your edges with my fingertips and spilled my every thought onto your cream coloured pages. Always my confidant, it seems melancholy that my journal has become my only confidant.

Months have passed by since our second wedding and now he has me all to himself. Oh, how I miss my family, my job... Vee.

This just isn't what I signed up for.

Losing myself,

Rose

Music played quietly in the reception room as the roaring fire warmed the space. It wasn't a particularly cold day outside but this grand old house tended to get a little chilly. Sasha leant over and selected a chocolate out of the box sitting on the reflective, gold lamp table next to the sofa. This is where she found herself sitting most days when Stella was with their newly appointed Nanny. As she slowly unwrapped the silver paper, she felt at ease. Keir was at work and the chocolates accompanied by a note was his latest tactic in smoothing things over.

'I love you' it said, 'let's not fight again.'

A simple yet meaningless message. Sasha knew that it would happen again. It wasn't a fight anyway, more him attacking her. She submitted, on the floor of their bedroom. Inside, Sasha was deeply unhappy, discontent with her life in London. Keir had coached her, moulded her into his almost perfect wife, who resembled nothing like Sasha; a once independent, free and driven young woman.

Meek and submissive were not in Sasha's vocabulary.

Until now.

Until she sat there, opening each little parcel of sugary goodness and eating them one by one. As Sasha continued to devour all twelve chocolates, she became lost in thought as a wave of self-guided amnesia flowed through her body. The smooth manoeuvre of Keir leaving her chocolates seemed to appease Sasha, who simply had fallen under his spell.

Suddenly, the doorbell chimed. It was the cleaner coming to take care of the house. It was during this time that Sasha continued to write, handwritten notes that she would keep in a box under the stairs. Keir would never look there, she thought, never wanting him to read the exposé of words she expressed.

'One day' she imagined, 'I'll be piecing the puzzle of my life back together. Then will come my book.'

It was a dream that she could barely envision yet writing her feelings down seemed to put her back together; ready for another round with Keir. So that afternoon, she sat at the dark stained desk in the corner of the room. With its gold accents, she felt truly special when she sat at this desk. As Keir had taken all technology away, apart from her phone, Sasha had no choice but to hand write as she had always done and it was a slow process. Yet still, she persevered, writing her meaningful prose as often as she could.

CHAPTER THIRTY-FIVE

It's all going to be Alright

It's getting worse.

He disconnected the house phone the other day. My phone, well it's been gone since the day he destroyed it, throwing it against the bathroom door where I wept.

He's not always like this, malevolent and cruel. Some days I see why I married him although those days seldom arrive.

Now as I retrieve every single fragment of our fractured life, I promise to try very hard to piece it back together.

Staying strong,
Rose

"Get upstairs now, you stupid bitch" he said, still calm yet injecting a cunning tone to his usually unruffled, English accent.

Sasha walked slowly up the stairs, peering back at Keir. Their eyes locked, and Sasha felt an uneasiness about her husband. He was angry about something and she couldn't figure out why.

There was nothing unusual about Keir's scathing words as unfortunately his abrupt outbursts were becoming more and more prevalent. Without a phone to call home, nor a computer to access the internet, Sasha's world had closed in and she hadn't yet formulated a way out of this mess.

By noon the next day, a bunch of 'apology flowers' would often arrive at the door and as each bunch would wilt, Sasha would feel even more disempowered; lost and out of touch.

"Darling, I'm sorry. You know how it is. I work in a hospital in the most ghastly situations. I promise things will be different now" he'd say this time.

A predictably similar story to the last.

Despite the apologies, the flowers and the chocolates, things between Keir and Sasha were getting worse. There was a time when she had a voice, a way to stand up to Keir's ever-evolving moods. As the years rolled on and Stella began school, Sasha would look in the mirror most mornings and cry. She no longer recognised the woman staring back at her, and blamed karma for her now trapped life. In a twisted way, Sasha thought she deserved it.

Those tears wouldn't continue to fall all day as Sasha was a mum, first and foremost. She did her best to shield Stella from the carnage of her marriage. Always first on her morning list would be to get Stella safely off to school. What would usually follow was a trip to the organic fruit and vegetable store to pick up Keir's ever-important fresh produce, as he would accept nothing less.

Today was no different.

As she returned home from her morning duties, Sasha placed her coat on the stand that stood left of the entrance inside their home.

'Peace' she thought, as she continued through to the kitchen.

Anytime that Keir wasn't home was Sasha's favourite time of day.

As she placed her grocery bags onto the stone countertop, Sasha noticed something.

There on the table was a pair of scissors. Beside the scissors was a note. As she approached, she realised that the note had been written by Keir, because of his very distinctive doctor-style handwriting.

She began to read.

'I noticed that you have been getting a lot of attention lately. Surprise me. A nice short haircut would do it. Don't disappoint.'

His words radiated down her spine. She had no idea what Keir was talking about.

'What attention?' she pondered.

Her whole body shook.

Not a moment passed and Sasha heard Keir walk through from the hall.

She froze. Unable to move or speak. Sasha knew he would force her to do this.

'He'll be in a bad mood' Sasha thought, and before she could move, in walked Keir, home early that morning from the hospital.

"So, you got my note?" he asked, smugly.

"Yes" Sasha said.

"But there is no way I'm cutting my hair!"

Her defiance seemed to spark an intense glare from Keir.

"Are we going to do this the easy way, or the hard way?" he said, crossing his arms.

Sasha gulped, scared yet there she stood with poise.

"No. I won't do it."

Hearing her refusal made Keir step forward.

He wasn't budging and as he reached over to take the scissors, Sasha quickly stood in front of them, shielding them from his view.

"Do it" he said, intently.

"We are not leaving this room until it's done."

Twenty-two minutes passed and Sasha couldn't handle it anymore.

'It's only hair' she told herself.

As Sasha took that first cut, she felt like she was cutting little chunks of her soul away.

'I hate you' she said internally, staring her monster of a husband in the eye.

Cutting her hair to just above her shoulders seemed to appease Keir. Sasha wept as she did it, feeling her long locks drop quickly to the floor. It wasn't perfect yet Keir was happy. He stood there with such authority, and as Sasha finished her impromptu haircut, she gathered her shortened locks up into a petite ponytail.

"There. Are you happy?" she said, staring at Keir with glassy eyes.

She knew that his control over her had grown and that whether she liked it or not, Keir wasn't going to return to that man she once knew. Despite being seemingly able to leave the house, Sasha didn't feel all that free at all.

CHAPTER THIRTY-SIX

Monster in the closet

He found my box of journals and tossed them up in the attic. So here I sit, at my desk writing on the back of an old phone bill. This is one part of me he cannot touch. I will write, and I will use my inner voice to fight. He may have left me beaten, as a hollow woman with barely a will to live. If it were not for my daughter, I would go. I would run and I would hide.

Keir, if you find this piece of paper, go ahead. Take your best shot.

This shadow you have created will come to life again — you just wait and see.

Here, but not,

Rose.

That very next day, Keir let Sasha take Stella to school. One thing Sasha knew for sure was that she could not run. Keir had convinced her of that. Despite having moments where she saw a chance for an imminent escape, those thoughts would quickly diminish and Sasha would retreat inside herself, believing Keir's words; allowing them to cut her, right through to her core. Keir could be sweet one minute, and a monster the next and for this reason, Sasha secretly nicknamed him her monster in the closet.

Deep inside, she had a secret that played on her mind. That time she betrayed Claire. Those moments, where reality was thrown out the window and replaced with careless passion. Days when all that mattered was James.

That little voice inside Sasha's head would retell the story; of a self-indulging time that went on and on selfishly, until Claire passed away and finally the guilt caught up. Sasha felt that her life now was really a reflection of what she deserved; karma had come and although she desperately wanted a new life with Stella, she could barely envision what it would look like. Her memories of that time, and the emotional abuse coming from Keir caused Sasha to almost bury any hope she had. Yet still, her truth shone bright, through her writing; the better side to her inner voice.

Another year had passed, and not a whole lot had changed. Sasha was still beaten down emotionally. One positive, was that Keir was spending more and more time at work. Her freedom was still limited yet this extra time away from Keir afforded her the luxuries of spending more time at Stella's school helping in the classroom and taking the short walk home by a local green. This is where she felt a surge of freedom reminiscent of times back home in Australia. A place where Sasha would play freely with Stella – kicking a ball and playing games.

As a protective mum, Sasha had built an imaginary wall up around Stella and herself; a separate world that Keir could not penetrate. A mother-daughter relationship that was intensely close; a bond that no person, not even Keir could break. To Sasha, this was purely a tactic as she knew that as Stella would grow, a strong relationship with her mother would be important. Especially if one day they would escape the deep-cutting restraints of a life bound in fear.

When he was home, Keir was impossible to live with. His moods would vary, from that sweet and kind man she met in Australia to a dreadful, pain-provoking monster who used his presence as a weapon. The never-ending taunts about her ability to be a mother, a wife and a woman in general continued to remove all trace of the old Sasha; that free-spirited country girl with big dreams.

The wall she had built between them would still waiver at times as Keir would fire words like bullets into her heart. Stella never bore the brunt of Keir's outbursts so Sasha knew that the best times were always the days where Stella was home, playing in the garden or running through the house. It was obvious to Sasha that Stella was very important to Keir and to remove her would ruin him. Sasha wanted nothing more than to take Stella and run. Yet still, somehow, Keir convinced her that in running she would fail. Sasha could never provide the way Keir could – financially at least. Here they stood, in their multi-million-pound property, with a world of belongings. The best of everything. Yet inside those walls live a family in turmoil, all down to one man.

"Go upstairs and change that dress" he would say to Sasha, suggesting that it wasn't appropriate to wear out for dinner.

Like a loyal dog, she would do as he said. Moments later, Sasha would reappear, wearing something a little more modest, more to Keir's liking. He would take her out to work dinners and whisper in her ear.

"Smile, like the beautiful woman you are."

To some women this would be a compliment. To Sasha, it made her skin crawl.

He wanted a handbag not a wife, Sasha thought.

Keir would swan her around these get togethers mimicking that they were the perfect couple, talking about their daughter followed by trips they would never take.

"We are really looking forward to spending some time in Australia next year" he would say, referencing the beautiful beaches and glorious fresh seafood.

His colleagues ate it right up, taking in every word as gospel. He made it seem like they were happy; a concept that Sasha couldn't even imagine anymore. They were far from happy and for as long as they would remain together, nothing would ever change that.

Function after function, Sasha would cry on the inside. She knew not to show her emotions and embarrass Keir, for the reaction later wouldn't be worth the tears. One evening, at the hospital's annual Christmas party, Sasha realised something.

There was a way out.

It was going to be difficult, yet there was an exit; just waiting for her to take it. If only she could get a moment alone with Dr. Swatsky, Keir's supervisor. She could tell him everything and maybe, just maybe he would listen.

Dr. Swatsky could help her escape.

As quickly as hope would come, it would diminish. Keir took Sasha home, relieved the Nanny and quickly morphed back into the monster in the closet.

That night, Sasha dreamt of leaving with Stella. She wondered how her family was. If they missed her and if they'd been trying to get in touch. It had been so long since Sasha had heard their voices. Had they forgotten her? She thought, truly removed from all reality.

Taking the trek to school, albeit short, gave Sasha a time to bond with her daughter by herself, away from the judgemental eye of Keir. The open air felt freeing and despite Stella often dragging her feet, it was Sasha's most favourite part of the day. They would walk and talk, and play little games along the way. Like, their very own version of eye spy and other fun games. As Sasha reached the school gate, she would rarely walk in these days as miss independent Stella was confident to make her way to her classroom without worry. This particular day was not as cold as the last and so at the gate, Sasha stopped there to watch Stella skip off toward the cluster of buildings. Her long and perfect pigtails bounced on top of her school bag as she made her way to a group of friends, awaiting Stella's arrival. She was a popular young student who despite her parent's problems, seemed very happy and carefree; much like her mother was as a child. Always fun and vibrant, Stella made Sasha very proud to be her Mum.

'You are just the most beautiful girl in the world'

Sasha thought, watching her daughter run off with her friends. Little Stella waved and shared a smile with her mother as she disappeared in between the big, old heritage school buildings. Catching Sasha's eye as she went to look away, was a man kissing his daughter on the forehead and sending her on her way. She had not noticed this gentleman before and she wondered why! Here he was; attractive and probably very married! Thought Sasha.

"Hot Dad alert!" said a familiar voice coming from behind.

Sasha spun around, and was greeted by Tess, the mother of one of Stella's good friends.

"I don't know what you're talking about!" snapped Sasha, in a sassy tone and with an equally cheeky grin across her face.

Sasha knew exactly what Tess was talking about. The view from the school gate seemed a lot more exciting than usual.

"His name is Alex. I can tell you were wondering!" commented Tess.

"I wasn't wondering!" said Sasha. "I was just admiring the view!"

Tess went onto tell Sasha that Alex was actually very single, a widower with two young daughters who had just started at the school. He had moved to the city for work, and had come from Wiltshire.

"Too bad you've already got your knight in shining

armour!" piped Tess, unaware of Keir's alter ego.

Little did Tess know that Sasha wasn't really living a fairy tale life.

"He's just a guy dropping his daughters off at school. I am far from interested" said Sasha, with surety.

Tess laughed.

"Sasha, you might be married, but you're also human! There's nothing wrong with admiring this glorious view" said Tess, doing just that.

There she stood, with her hand on one hip, watching with anticipation as Alex began to walk toward them.

Sasha nervously shielded her face.

"Did he hear us?" she said, totally freaking out at the thought that this handsome man was coming on over.

All Tess could do was laugh.

"Hey, I'm single and ready to mingle... I just didn't think it'd happen at the school gate!" a quick-witted Tess joked.

With his dark hair and fit physique, he walked on over with a grin from ear to ear.

"Hi ladies, would either of you like to buy a ticket in the school raffle? We're trying to raise some funds for new sports equipment" he explained.

Sasha felt relieved that he wasn't coming over to catch the pair out.

"Oh sure" said Tess, quickly handing over some loose change.

Still a little mesmerised by his by his incredibly good looks, Sasha didn't quite get the question.

"He wants to know if you want to buy a ticket, Sasha. You seem distracted?" teased Tess.

"Oh yes. Of course," Sasha said nervously, scrambling for her purse.

"Oh, I don't have any coins. Can I bring it to school this afternoon?"

"Sure!" Alex said, without delay.

"Let's meet here."

That afternoon as she reached the school gate, Sasha peered around for Alex, hoping to run into the handsome single dad. It didn't take long to spot him, walking up the path toward the gate.

"Hi! I didn't catch your name before" he said, approaching Sasha, with his right hand out, ready to greet her.

"My name is Sasha. I'm Stella's Mum. I think one of your daughters are in her class" she said.

Alex smiled, introducing himself.

"Yes, Scarlett's class I believe! I'm Alex. Alex Potter" he said, "it's so lovely to meet you."

A slight delay of silence followed as Sasha counted some coins and handed them to Alex for the raffle tickets.

"That will buy you three, just pop your name down here and you'll be right to go" he said, with a friendly smile.

"Thanks, I'll see you again soon."

He turned to walk toward the classrooms.

It wouldn't be too long and Sasha would be spending more time with Mr. Alex Potter.

CHAPTER THIRTY-SEVEN

Making the Most of Things

I think I'm addicted to men.

But Alex is my friend. Not my lover.

He is fun and we laugh. It's nothing more.

Harmlessly making friends again,

Rose

“Could you please cut me a piece of tape?” Alex asked, holding two pieces of paper firmly between his fingers.

“I'm determined to make this the most successful cake stall our little school has ever seen!” he said, with gusto.

Sasha and Alex had volunteered to setup a special stand to display delicious homemade treats made by parents. Money raised was to go toward Alex's plight to bring new sports equipment into the school.

They continued chatting, over the echoing sounds of children's voices coming from the neighbouring classrooms.

"I'm sure it'll be amazing. Hordes of kids and parents will be lining up in no time!" said Sasha, easing Alex's concerns.

"So where in Australia are you from?" he asked, inquisitively.

"I grew up on a farm in country New South Wales."

Her answer, short and sweet.

Alex quizzed her further and before long he had her sharing stories of growing up with her sister and reminiscing about how much she missed them all so much.

"It's been years since I've been home. Stella was just a baby when I last set foot in Australia."

Alex looked stunned when Sasha said this.

"So, you're saying, you haven't seen or talked to your family in all this time?" he asked, undeniably concerned.

Sasha took a breath and hesitantly told Alex that Keir preferred it this way.

"There was no fight, nor disagreements. We just fell out of touch" she said, trying to keep her emotions at bay.

In a way, Sasha was trying to tell Alex that Keir was behind all of this, yet without really telling him everything.

"Here" said Alex, pulling his phone from his back pocket.

"Call your family."

Sasha realised that she'd indeed shared a little too much.

Alex began to put the pressure on.

"Sasha, if you're in trouble, you need to tell me. I won't judge. I'll only help you" he said, edging closer, placing his hand gently on her forearm.

"I'm okay. I really am! Thanks for the offer to use your phone but there are phones everywhere that I can use" she said, trying to somehow explain herself out of this conversation.

Alex then lent in to caress Sasha's face, tilting her head up to look him in the eye.

"Always know you deserve better, Sasha. I can help you if you're scared."

Within seconds, she began to feel her emotions getting the better of her. So, instead of becoming an imminent blubbering mess, she picked up her purse and left.

Rushing out through the gate, she felt a cage close in around her. With every hurried step she took, Sasha was feeling further trapped. So, she began to run.

'I need to get home, fast' she thought, as a barrage of tears flowed down her face.

Arriving home was bittersweet. This house was a prison. It was never much of a home. Sasha was drowning and if she wasn't going to leave now, when would she? It was time, she thought, and before she could think up another move, in strolled Keir, dressed in his robe and clasping a cup of tea in his hands.

He was home.

"How was school?" Keir asked, surprisingly in a more upbeat tone than usual.

"It was good" Sasha said, as she removed her coat.

"Who is Alex?" asked Keir who had followed her into the front room.

"What?" she said, shocked that Keir knew anything about her friend.

"Who is Alex? I said."

Keir's voice deepened.

"He's just a parent from school who was helping today" answered Sasha, hesitantly.

A moment of silence followed.

"Turn and face me" instructed Keir.

Sasha did was she was told. He stared at her face and gently placed his cup of tea down onto a side table to his right.

"He called me today. You forgot that my phone number is down as the contact at school. What have I told you? Never disrespect me!"

Without warning, her husband leapt toward Sasha, pushing her with force. She fell, and went crashing through the glass coffee table that sat behind her.

Her head, bounced down onto the sofa.

Sasha shrieked.

"Stop! Leave me alone!" she bellowed, feeling pain throughout her entire body.

"Don't you dare disrespect me again" Keir said, pointing at his wife and standing over her frightened shell.

After picking herself up, Sasha remembered the time. She was shaking and injured yet knew that school was ending in just a short couple of hours. Keir had vanished into another room and so Sasha made her way upstairs. First, to assess her injuries and second, to shower away any remnants of glass that may have lodged into her body.

As she stood naked inside the shower of her locked bathroom, Sasha got brave. She wanted out of this hell.

After quickly drying off and changing, she retreated to the guest room. Sasha had spent enough time in this room to know that below the window was a garden wall that may have been accessible enough to aide in her escape.

Leaping from the window ledge, Sasha bravely balanced along the wall and plunged down into the garden below. She had a way to go, yet escaping had to happen and now was the time to do it. This was perfect timing as Stella was at school. Keir was still downstairs. His control over Sasha was so immense now that Sasha had completely lost her identity. The only places he would allow her to go was to the school, grocery store and home. She knew that since he'd heard from Alex, things were only going to get worse.

'This isn't the way it was supposed to be' Sasha thought often, yet these kinds of thoughts would come and they would go.

Keir's control was more prevalent than ever so Sasha knew that the moment she felt as brave as she did right now, was the moment to leap out of that open window. She had no care for her belongings and nothing felt like it was truly hers anyway. Keir not only ran her life, he ran the entire house. It never truly felt like home to Sasha. At least since the day he snapped, the day their baby girl came home.

As she tiptoed through the garden, she braced herself as she looked at the tall fence beyond. Sasha knew that her neighbour, Betsy being end of terrace had a side gate. All Sasha had to do was climb that fence and get through that gate. However, she knew freedom was still a dash away, up to the school where Stella was and to the hospital to speak with Dr. Swatsky. Time was ticking and it wouldn't be long until Keir would be on the hunt for his wife. The prison he had created for Sasha had been compromised and he was bound to be upset.

Sasha placed her right foot onto the fence ledge and began her climb. She made it to the very top and dropped down the other side, scraping herself as she fell. Sasha was okay and ran quickly toward the gate.

It was locked. Sasha was trapped. Betsy's Cocker Spaniel, alerted to the noise and barked her way. With her empowered heart pumping through her chest and her tears on standby, Sasha frantically ran around, searching for an exit.

She tried the back door of Betsy's terrace.

There was no answer and the door was locked.

Darting her eyes up and down the fence, she found it! Her exit in the distance. Right in the back corner of Betsy's garden was a summer house which would provide ample leverage for Sasha to climb up and over the side fence.

That side fence would take her onto the street.

As she ran over towards the corner of the garden, with Betsy's dog running at her feet, Sasha noticed something even more valuable; a ladder. It was leaning up against the summer house. She lifted the old, rusty ladder, brushing the spider webs away. Sasha lent it up against the sturdy fence and climbed up and as she got her leg over the edge, there he was. Standing there, with a stern look on his face and still wearing his robe.

"Keir" she said, with fear and trepidation in her voice.

Sasha was shaking.

"I saw you from the window" he said, in his usual calm and soul-shaking tone.

"Get home. Now." Keir said deeply, creating a kind of fear in Sasha that took her own voice away. She swallowed back the part of her that got her to this point. That overwhelming sense of bravery buried itself back deep into her gut. It diminished, leaving Sasha just a shell of a woman, fearing for her life.

Keir helped his wife down from the fence and cupped her hand tightly. As they walked around the corner toward home, no words were spoken. The only communication was a smile at a stranger walking his dog. Sasha feared what was to come, a punishment she imagined as they walked toward their front door. The crimson colour of the door, matched the mood of both Keir and Sasha. Sasha was scared, like bone tingling scared. What would he take from her this time? What was left? She pondered.

As he closed the red front door, a devilish look adorned his face. He stared her down, so far down that she fell onto the wooden floor. Taking his finger and pointing it at her teary face, Keir said the most hurtful words yet.

"If you walk out on me, Sasha. You leave Stella behind."

And with that, he secured the house and then sat down in his chair. All the while Sasha sat shaking, waiting for instruction. He had torn her to shreds. Here sat a woman in fear, scorned by a man who she used to love.

That day, Keir accompanied Sasha to the school gate in a stance of unity. Alex saw the pair and dared not to approach. This was Sasha's reality and escaping now seemed even more impossible.

CHAPTER THIRTY-EIGHT

A Familiar Face

He's letting me out of the house alone again. So that's been nice. Though, his mood is still like a rollercoaster, yet somehow, I'm surviving.

Just existing, really.

Missing home,
Rose

Through the crowd, Sasha saw a familiar face and before she could get a better look, that face became harder and harder to visualise.

'It can't be!' she thought as she glanced a little harder at the face in the crowd.

Sasha had been out doing a spot of shopping before it was time to collect Stella from school.

'J?' she thought, as the face disappeared. If it were James, he sure was a long way from home.

Sasha made her way through the barrage of people, pushing through with both her arms swinging from side to side. The swarm of people were absolutely covering the square. She could see the back of James' head as he continued on in the other direction. Desperately wanting to see that face again, Sasha powered through the people, without any thought to her surroundings. This was all she wanted; a little piece of home. And there he was, in London.

'How could this be?' she thought, but barely, whilst keeping her eye on the prize.

"Stop!" she called, although the sounds coming from the people drowned out her voice.

Sasha tripped, but regained her balance, still following James' elusive footsteps.

As she made it out the other side, she stood there, gazing around. Sasha had lost sight of him and there seemed to be a thousand other men looking fairly similar.

"James!" she called, as she panned around, in search of her old love.

Where could he be? She thought. Was it really him?

Her eyes locked. There he was. The man she saw in the crowd. He was now sitting on a bench seat chatting to another guy.

It wasn't James after all.

Sasha sighed in disappointment. For a moment there, she had this romantic notion in her head that he had chased her to London. What foolish thought.

Walking back toward where she started, Sasha felt defeated. She wanted it desperately, to see James again. And not only James. Her family. Those who she left behind. Part of Sasha feared contacting them again, especially her father. Yet she couldn't seem to wrap her head around why they hadn't tried searching for her.

Her family knew her address. Not even a letter had ever arrived, just to say hello.

CHAPTER THIRTY-NINE

The Truth Comes Out

I often wonder how you are, Dad. If you're safe and well. I've let you down for staying away for so long. Even if I could leave and return to Australia, would you even know who I am now?

Keir had our passports locked in a safe until the other day. When he gave me back mine and refused me access to Stella's. He knows I'll never leave my daughter behind.

I'm sorry Dad. I miss you so much and I want you back in my life. Though I must choose my child. She needs me.

Longing for you,
Rose

"I can't believe what I'm reading!" Sasha whispered as she sat idle in the attic.

She had climbed up to find her box of old journals whilst Keir was at work.

Sasha had found them, strewn across the room. Although, their contents were much less intriguing than the box Sasha had just torn open. She had found it in the very corner of the room, under the eaves. In that box contained what was likely to be the biggest secret Keir had kept from his wife.

As Sasha scurried through the news clippings and remnants of his past, she felt like she had been hit with a bat.

Matilda had been murdered.

Furthermore, she had been killed in the very house that Keir had 'bought' for he and Sasha.

Her discovery knocked the wind from her lungs. As she read on, she learned that there had been some kind of home invasion and that a botched robbery seemed to be the cause.

Concerned that Keir could come home at any moment, Sasha quickly placed the box back under the eaves and surrounded it with others, disguising that she had tampered with it. Before climbing down the ladder, Sasha slid a single news clipping into her pocket for later reading.

Her fear around what her husband may have done shrouded every bone in her body.

'Could he be responsible? she thought, wondering if Matilda had been a victim of his abuse as well.

Perhaps things had escalated.

Sasha no longer had a choice. Escaping this life with Stella had to happen and she made it her goal to get home to Australia. To see her father, if he was still alive, and to be close with her sister again.

CHAPTER FORTY

The Great Escape

Tonight, marks the last evening I will
spend serving this man, living this lie.

I will not face another day of his
torment and abuse. My daughter will be
safe, and so will I.

Fighting for life, in the purest kind.
Waiting for the day I get to say, 'I'm free'.

Going home without a doubt,
Rose

W aking in a sweat from an intense dream, Sasha
relived it momentarily as she lay alone in her
bed. Keir, like most mornings was still at
work and she knew today was the day.

Her dream had moved her; evoked a part of her core
that had been destroyed by Keir. It had brought life to an
issue she hadn't faced for a while; her need and desire to
escape. Her mother had visited in her dream and shared
words that shook Sasha deeply. Maggie was not gentle in
her approach when she told Sasha that she did not

approve of her packaging her life up and giving it to Keir. Sasha's mother said that it was not a time to wallow, it was a time to thrive. It was now or never, she said, Stella deserved a better life.

And so did Sasha.

There she lay, after years of abuse with a deep realisation that this no longer made any sense. Whether she ended up back here or not, attempting to escape was worth every risk.

So, with that, Sasha used it to fuel her desire to leave. Once and for all. Instantly, she knew what she needed to do; go to the hospital. She'd need to avoid Keir and meet with Dr. Swatsky.

It was the only way out of this turmoil. She didn't have Stella's passport and zero chance of getting out without help. At this point, Sasha understood that Keir's actions were not of a rational man. He had problems and she knew that Dr Swatsky would help him. Her plan was not without risk though, as she truly did not know how the doctor would react. She hoped, more than anything, that he would see it too, that Keir needed professional help.

So, as she quickly dressed that day, she looked around her house one more time. It was quite likely that upon leaving, she would never see inside it again. Despite the pain caused within its walls, it was home for a time. It was the place she brought her daughter to upon leaving hospital and there were happy memories; early on.

'Please, stay strong. Stay fierce. Be as tough as your

mother, Sasha' she said to herself, as she took one last glance into the mirror above the side table in the hall.

Grasping Stella's hand tight, she walked out, locking the door behind her. Only a small duffle bag of belonging swung over her arm. In a way, it didn't sound rational, going straight into the mouth of the dragon. Though somehow Sasha always thought that going to Dr. Swatsky would be the most sensible way out.

After leaving, she had not explained to Stella what was going on. Yet it was clear that Sasha wasn't being as subtle as she perhaps had hoped.

Stella was asking questions and Sasha was vague, not answering to Stella's satisfaction.

"Mum! I'm not coming then!" Stella proclaimed, in a stubborn and abrupt tone.

"If I'm not going to school, where are we going?"

Sasha looked down at her daughter, and knelt at her height.

She cleared her throat.

"We are going to get help for Dad."

Stella continued with her mother, running across the street to catch a nearby taxi. Sasha never drove in London as Keir wouldn't ever allow such freedom. So, it was either taxi cabs, the tube or walking; her only ways of transport.

They got into the black vehicle, and Sasha asked to be taken to the hospital. In the car, Stella rested on Sasha's stomach, feeling close to her anxious mum. This helped, as Sasha's nerves were rampantly high. It felt like the longest car trip ever, as her thoughts were going faster than the speed of the car. She knew that her courage was often fleeting, yet she had come this far. Never had Sasha been this close to freedom before. She found herself imagining embracing her sister again and all of what that meant. She was so close. It was now or never, she thought, as the taxi drew closer to the hospital buildings afar.

A few minutes passed, as the taxi stopped, close to the entrance. She paid the driver and got out of the car. She stopped for a moment, grabbing her daughter's hand tight. The building was so broad, and Sasha had no idea where to find Dr. Swatzky.

Summoning her inner strength again, she felt an innate urge to speak to her mother. Although Sasha couldn't hear her voice, she could feel a warmth surround her that winter's day. The heat beaming from nowhere evoked the strength she needed to march into that building and demand change; fight for her daughter and their freedom.

'I can do this' she told herself, and with that she heard her mother's voice.

"You *can* do this."

It took her twenty-four minutes to find Dr. Swatzky's office, on the 3rd floor of the towering hospital. After talking her way through a barrage of other staff, she finally knocked on his door.

"Come in" he said, and without delay Sasha let him

know everything, and presented the doctor with the news clipping she had found.

A feeling of release dawned over her as Dr. Swatsky agreed to help. He admitted that Keir's odd behaviour at times concerned him and hearing Sasha's version of events only set his fears in concrete.

"I'll ensure you and your daughter are safe" he said, before calling for help.

"All I want is to go home to Australia with Stella" Sasha explained and with that, Dr. Swatsky said he'd do all he could to make that happen.

CHAPTER FORTY-ONE

It's over

We did it!

Dr. Swatsky made Keir agree to let us leave.

As I stood quietly looking over my defeated husband in his hospital bed, he admitted everything. Keir couldn't hold it in anymore. He killed Matilda and he says it was an accident. His mental illness 'made him do it.' I guess his mental illness made him do a lot of things.

Ultimately, he wanted Stella to be safe. I don't care whether he ever loved me or not. He loves Stella. He wants her safe and that's one thing we can agree on.

I can never forgive him for what he has done to me, nor should I have to.

Flying home to Australia,
Rose

“Here we are” Sasha beamed, as she and Stella stepped off the bus.

They only had to walk about five-hundred metres to the gates of Maggie Creek.

With no clue as to what lie ahead up the old dirt track, Sasha felt uneasy. Her future, still unknown. Making their way to the farm's entrance and down the beaten, old track, Sasha concentrated on making her daughter feel at ease. They danced, they sung and spun around, flinging the dirt from their shoes.

"See beautiful? This is what I've been telling you about!" explained Sasha, pointing out into the paddocks beyond.

"It's so hot here Mum!" commented Stella, still becoming acclimatised to the hotter weather. It was February after all.

"We're nearly there" assured her mum as they reached the bend in the road.

"There it is!"

Sasha guided her daughter's eyes toward the farmhouse and instantly noticed something different. There was their old family home, painted and looking quite beautiful. The old tin shed had been torn down and replaced with a newer, American style barn.

Her anticipation turned to disappointment. Clearly this wasn't the Maggie Creek she remembered.

"Dad mustn't live here anymore" Sasha said, lowering her voice.

They'd come so far and with that, decided to approach the house anyway. Off in the distance, sat the old white cottage on top of the hill.

'Oh, the memories' Sasha thought, before knocking on the new screen door.

As she waited, she inhaled the air. It smelt the same as Sasha remembered so in a way this old place hadn't changed too much.

Soon, without much warning, the screen door flung open, almost knocking Sasha and Stella away.

"Sasha!" a voice said.

That voice was Jess, who pounced forward and squeezed her sister tight.

"Is this Stella? Oh my God."

Happy tears were shed that day and what welcome home it was. Sasha learned that after Frank had moved into a retirement home, Jess, Ally and their now two children had made a long-term home on the farm. Sasha learned that Jess had been conversing with who she thought was her sister in emails back and forth for years.

"You always had an excuse as to why you couldn't visit or video chat" she explained, after realising that it was Keir responding, not Sasha.

"I thought you wanted nothing to do with me" said Sasha, unable to fight back her tears.

"Never" said Jess.

"How could you ever think we could do that to you? We'd always hoped you'd come back some day."

"I guess my next question is, when did Dad pass?" Sasha reluctantly asked, falling into an emotional mess.

"Sash, he's alive! He's living in care and doesn't know Arthur to Martha, but he's still with us!"

Relief showered her once trampled body.

"I want to see him. As soon as I can. I want to him" she said, with delight.

CHAPTER FORTY-TWO

unconditional Love

Bravely, I stare forward. My eyes fixed on moving on. Freedom still feels foreign to me.

And as I now dance in the sun, I remember the storm. The days where I let myself believe that I deserved what I was getting. I fell into the trap of another, and came out the other side as a warrior. I'm just like my Mum. Strong. Fierce and ready to reach out and touch my dreams.

I will finish this book of reflection and then I will write another. And another. Until some day, I can safely say I've rose above the pain.

Finally free,
Rose

Arriving to see Frank for the first time in years, was difficult. He was now residing in an assisted living home in town because it was no longer safe for him to stay on the farm.

With Jess, Sasha quietly walked down the hall toward his room. It was a long corridor with doors to either side. Being lunch time, most residents were out eating in the dining room. Frank was one of them, though Jess wanted to show Sasha his room before he arrived back after lunch.

"Here it is" she explained, opening the door and stepping into his labyrinth of belongings.

"Dad keeps getting me to bring things in from the farm. To the nurse's disgust, he's really made himself at home!"

Sasha grinned, running her fingers across an old dresser that used to be in her parents' bedroom. That familiar smell of the old farm, filled the room and seeing Frank's old recliner sitting in the corner brought back many memories.

"I was worried about him living in some old sterile hospital room but this, this is great" said Sasha, happy to see some remnants of the past.

The sisters stood around chatting for a little while until they were met by a friendly Irish accent, a nurse who had been caring for Frank.

"Hi ladies. Jessica, Dad will be back shortly. Who do we have here?"

Jess introduced Sasha to Grace, who seemed like the friendliest nurse on the planet.

"I can tell you my dear Sasha that he has spoken your name and we have had some in-depth conversations about you over the past year."

'He's been here a year?' Sasha gasped, unaware that it had been so long.

"Yes, Frank has been a resident here for..." she paused, before looking at his chart.

"Our records say 13 months".

Sasha heard the words, yet a wave of accountability struck her down. She fell into an abyss of shock.

The tone and volume of Sasha's voice subdued, as she acknowledged Grace's words silently.

"Your father gets quite confused at times but be assured today is a good day."

Nurse Grace's words helped although the guilt of not being here still penetrated like a knife.

It's too late, she thought, wondering what Frank was thinking and feeling. Sasha desperately hoped that today was indeed a good day as she wasn't sure how she'd take it if her father didn't recognise her.

Sasha allowed her imagination to run wild, picturing her father sitting propped in a chair, being spoon fed his midday meal. Whether that was Frank's reality or not, this is how she envisioned her father now; a shell of the man he once was.

Soon, she would come to realise that this wasn't the case at all and as Frank hobbled in, now using a walking frame for support, Sasha nervously smiled.

"Hey Dad" greeted Jess.

"Look who I found loitering in the halls!"

Frank's face dropped.

"Sasha love. Come here darlin'!"

Relieved that she wasn't a stranger to him, Sasha rushed to hug her father.

From that moment on, they'd only ever be separated

by death. Sasha and young Stella would call the little white cottage on the hill their home, and the once independent woman she used to be would be reborn.

After returning to the farm following her visit, Sasha began to piece together her story, adding a short message within the first few pages of her novel.

May you smile more times than you frown,

Stand tall more times than you are down.

Be braver than the strongest, majestic knight,

And never let your dreams out of sight.

Be bold. Be proud. Be passionate.

And most of all,

Be you.

These words she found within one of her mother's journals. Maggie had recorded them the day before Sasha had moved to the city. Now a mother herself, Sasha could understand, on a deeper level, why these words were important. For life had dealt her quite the journey thus far, and this reminder from her mother was something she could pass down to Stella.

The rest of Sasha's story would come from the pages of her own old journals. A brave and sometimes harrowing journey of a woman who rose above it all.